Live and Die by the Gun

An Exciting Collection of Western Short Stories

William S. Hubbartt

Live and Die by the Gun

An Exciting Collection of Western Short Stories

By

William S. Hubbartt

William S. Hubbartt

Copyright Notice

The characters and events portrayed in this book are fictitious. Any similarity to real persons, living or dead, is coincidental and not intended by the author.

No part of this publication may be reproduced, stored in or introduced into a retrieval system, or transmitted, in any form, or by any means (electronic, mechanical, photocopying, recording, or otherwise), without the prior permission of the publisher, except by a reviewer who may quote brief passages in a review. Requests for permission should be directed to Permissions, William S. Hubbartt, PO Box, 1355, St. Charles, IL 60174.

The scanning, uploading, and distribution of this book via the Internet or via any other means without the permission of the publisher are illegal and punishable by law. Please purchase only authorized electronic or printed editions and do not participate in or encourage electronic piracy of copy-written materials.

Cover design by: Subinpamson - iStock 1163182067

Printed in the United States of America

© 2021, William S. Hubbartt

All Rights Reserved
ISBN-13: 9798708987747

Table of Contents

Hell and High Water She was kidnapped by Comanches; can a rancher save his wife? 1

Spirit Warrior Can a drifter and a Native woman with child survive on the trail? 17

Kokopelli's Serenade Does the spirit of Kokopelli foretell of new love or mischief? 26

The Hunted Deer hunters now become the hunted, will they survive?..36

Redemption Can a young gun find redemption from the accidental injury to a child? 44

Spanish Eyes Will a traveler find love in a cantina, or must he fight for his life? 52

The Spirit of Sonora Is it experience or a higher power that guides a young Texas Ranger? 59

Soldier's Heart Can a Captain overcome war stress to lead his troops in battle? 66

Dying Wish Will the townspeople honor the final request of their well-regarded sheriff? 71

Caleb's Courage Can a young soldier overcome his fears in the face of the enemy? 76

The Last Score How high are the stakes for simple train robbery? 82

Fool's Gold Released from prison, can a man re-start his life? 90

It Takes a Woman Will a mountain man who is trailing kidnappers succeed in rescuing a woman? 96

Death Sentence How will a gunslinger meet justice for his actions?..103

Donovan's Dream Will a California man succeed in finding the killer of his wife? 110

Selling Out Is there honor among thieves? 120

Publication credits 128
About the Author 129

Hell and High Water

She was kidnapped by Comanches; can a rancher save his wife?

"Hello, the ranch!"

Douglas turned quickly, his hand instinctively moving towards the heavy Paterson Colt that rested on his right hip. He cursed to himself for letting his guard drop while he fidgeted with the cinch as he saddled the dun. While the winter had been quiet, memories of the Comanche great raid of 1840 through central Texas a few short months ago lingered fresh. Inattention, even for a moment, could give the stealthy Comanche warriors the upper hand.

"Hello, the ranch," repeated the lone approaching rider, his right hand in the air as he halted his horse some fifty yards out. It was a customary precaution to announce one's presence and friendly intentions.

"Jake. Is that you?" asked Douglas. He now recognized the rider as a Ranger, one of the defenders employed by the Republic of Texas to patrol the plains against the criminal element as well as Native threats.

"Yep. Headin' back to Austin for the next assignment. You fixin' to ride to town?"

"Howdy Ranger Jake. Do you have time to stop for some coffee and fresh bread," asked Anna, Douglas' wife? A petite 19-year-old with blonde hair, Anna stepped out the doorway of the two-room mud and log shelter that was their home on the Texas prairie. "Or were you just planning on spiriting my husband away to go carousing in town?"

Jake smiled and touched his hat. "Morning Ma'am. Appreciate the offer. Captain's orders to get to Austin. Next time I pass through."

The 25-year-old rancher kissed his wife goodbye and then the two men headed east along the Colorado River trail towards Austin where Douglas intended to purchase a horse and supplies with plans to return the next day. The young couple had moved to Texas to take over the operation of the ranch after Anna's brother, Thomas, had died fighting Comanches at the battle of Plum Creek the previous fall.

Anne busied herself with sweeping out their dirt floor prairie home, and then, working at a small outside table, she began cleaning and skinning a wild turkey that Douglas had shot earlier in the morning. The feathers were making a mess, so she stepped into the house to find a small bag. Feathers blew across the doorway as she stepped out again. Suddenly from behind, a firm hand grabbed her by the mouth and jerked her back and she felt the sharp point of a knife at her throat. The smell of a sweaty body and the feel of a hard uncovered chest and copper-colored muscular arms about her meant that she had been captured by a Native warrior.

Little Bear, so named because of his short stocky build came around the corner of the log house, with a turkey feather dangling from his headband and one in his hand. On seeing the yellow-haired white woman tightly held by his tall lean companion, Running Horse, Little Bear gave a joyful yelp. He reached out with the feather to tickle the nose of the woman. Anne squirmed to turn away and gasped from the effort. Little Bear then grabbed at her dress.

Anna kicked at his reaching hand and then tried to twist out of the tight grip of the tall warrior. Running Horse squeezed the petite woman tighter, and she screamed when the knife nicked the skin under her chin. Now afraid for her life, and even more dreading the humiliation of being ravaged by the warriors, Anna swung her arm at the man in front of her and stomped her shoe onto the toe of her captor, and squealed a grunt of effort as she broke free and ran.

Hell and High Water

Running Horse dove after the fleeing woman, catching her long dress, which partially ripped away in his hands. She stumbled, losing her shoe, and the bottom hem of the dress tore free exposing her white ankles and calves as she fell, cutting her knee on a rock. The warriors laughed as they tackled this yellow-haired woman with spunk.

It was late afternoon the following day when Douglas approached the ranch, newly purchased horse in tow packed with supplies. Fluffy clouds hung in the sky and shadows stretched across the yard as the sun approached the western horizon. The log house and yard seemed surprisingly quiet. A crow cawed, and Douglas saw a flutter of wings as two blackbirds hopped about arguing over a morsel on the outdoor cutting table. A straw broom lay angled across the doorway threshold.

Douglas reined his horse to a stop, as the hair on his neck tingled. Watching for any movement, he reached for the Colt and cocked the hammer. The crows continued their tussle. Small white feathers drifted along the ground in the breeze near the cutting table.

"Anna,…Anna,… are you there? Are you all right?"

Dropping the lead for the supply horse, Douglas nudged his horse ahead cautiously. He circled towards the cutting table at the side of the house and saw a few scraps from the turkey he had shot the day before. Ants swarmed over the table and short feathers were scattered across the yard. Something was wrong, Anna would never leave a mess like this.

"Anna,…Anna,… Where are you?"

Douglas quickly scanned the yard and the horizon, seeing only empty Texas plains. He dismounted and crept stealthily towards the doorway. Silence hung in the air. A lonesome wind blew, fluttering the curtains Anna had used to decorate the kitchen window. Anticipation and fear grew. Could she have walked down to the creek? Could she be hurt? He spun quickly into the log home, gun first. Their few belongings were tossed about, and the Kentucky rifle was not in its normal corner. He felt goosebumps of fear on his skin.

Douglas rushed out of the house and circled the small log and mud structure, freezing instantly after a few steps. There on the ground, lay a torn fabric, the hem apparently ripped from Anna's dress. Then he saw a rock stained brown with blood, drag marks in the dirt, and a few yards up, Anna's shoes lay carelessly about. He followed the drag marks to the back of the house where he saw hoof prints. Unshod ponies! The Comanches have taken Anna!

Fear raced through his mind. Douglas recalled the story of how the Comanches had taken little Cynthia Parker, several years before. The little girl had never been found; rumor was they had raised her as their own. And there were stories about how the Natives ravaged and mistreated the white women they captured. The pony tracks lead northwest, towards the Comancheria, the Comanche homeland. Anger and determination swelled within. Douglas ran back to pack supplies. He would track these red devils and bring back his wife.

Running Horse had tied Anna's wrists tightly with a strip of rawhide, mounted his horse, and dragged her along like he was leading a stubborn mule. Angered by the death of his brother at the battle of Plum Creek, this young brave was anxious for revenge against the white man.

Little Bear followed along, laughing and taunting her, as she tried to run along keeping pace with the spotted pony. Her shoes had fallen off quickly and now her feet were becoming bloodied, running barefoot across the prairie. When she stumbled and fell she was dragged until Running Horse stopped his pony to let her stand. The prairie tall grass cut her legs as she ran along and then scratched her face and arms when she fell. She cried, begging them to stop, but the warriors laughed and kicked their ponies to continue. It had only been a mile or two, but to Anna, it seemed to be forever. She was weakening and falling more frequently, and then she twisted her ankle and fell hard screaming in pain, cutting her knee on a sharp stone, the wound bleeding onto the dry ground.

"Just kill me," she cried, and then, in anger, she grabbed a stone with her bound hands and tried to throw it at Running Horse.

Hell and High Water

"She still has fight in her," said Little Bear, in his native language.

"Yes," laughed Running Horse, replying in the Comanche tongue, "but we have three suns ride. I don't want to leave all that fight here on the prairie. I will show my prize to the elders, and bring a slave for my wife. I will let yellow hair ride for a while."

Running Horse yanked on the rawhide binding and pulled Anna up to his horse. He reached down and lifted Anna up like a small child, placing her on the horse, in front of him. In a flash, he had his knife at her throat.

"Ride now,…no fight," he said in heavy accented English, gesturing threateningly with his knife. Anna nodded submissively.

The afternoon sun had moved behind cloud cover. Dark storm clouds loomed in the distant western sky ahead.

Douglas quickly packed supplies needed for a week on the trail including balls, powder food, and coffee. He checked for and found his two flintlock pistols that were stored in a hidden cubby in the bedroom. He stored the remaining supplies and then stepped out, to ready the horses, but cursed to himself upon seeing that the sun had dropped below the horizon, leaving barely a half-hour of dusk remaining in the day. There was a crescent moon rising in the east; it would be too dark to follow a track. Reluctantly, Douglas decided to delay his departure until morning when he could see the trail.

He led the horses to their stalls in the covered shelter, rubbed them down from the day's ride, and then let them settle in for the night so that they would be fresh for riding in the morning. He forced himself to eat some dried beef, washed down with coffee, as the thoughts and fears in his mind raged in a tug-o-war between plans for finding Anna and fears for her well-being. Though sleep was desperately needed, he likely would not sleep tonight.

A tinge of gray began to lighten the eastern horizon as Douglas readied his horses for the day's journey. It had been a fitful night, with occasional periods of sleep disturbed by dreams of wife Anna fighting against an onslaught of painted warriors. Douglas had awakened several times in a sweat, feeling his arms swinging at imaginary foes.

The tracks were clear in the sandy-colored soil outside his door where it appeared Anna was dragged by the abductors, and around back to where they had mounted and then continued to drag her as she tried to run along behind two unshod ponies. It was obvious that Anna had stumbled and fallen and was dragged by her captors. Soon there was evidence of blood, showing injuries to her feet as she tried to keep pace. His anger quickly boiled over from seeing the tracks showing the horrible treatment of his wife. Douglas squeezed the saddle horn with his right hand as he fought the urge to scream in an uncontrolled fury, holding back the urge to race his horse in pursuit. "I must be calm, in control. I will get her. I will get them," the sound surprised Douglas as his thoughts transformed into words that came from his mouth.

He followed the trail for an hour, and finally, he observed that the dragging and bloodied footprints stopped. Worried, he dismounted and walked around in a circle looking carefully, but didn't see Anna's body. Ahead the pony tracks continued, but one horse showed a heavier imprint, like that of carrying extra weight from riding double. Soon the ponies' tracks stretched out to a canter, and likewise, Douglas picked up his pace.

The sunny sky began to turn gray as high clouds covered the sun. The wind had picked up slightly and now smelled of dampness, of rain. In the distance, to the northwest, dark clouds roiled. There were flashes of lightning in the clouds, with an occasional bolt to the ground. The breeze rattled the tall grass, which was still yellow and dry from the long winter. His horse snorted and side-stepped slightly suggesting its preference to turn back rather than continue into the tempest brewing in the distance. Determined to find his wife, Douglas held the reins tightly and nudged his horse forward.

Douglas' eyes caught movement ahead to the left. He put his rifle to his shoulder and sighted towards a running animal. There were two deer, they passed to his left with long bounding leaps. Then there was movement on the right; he swung his rifle in that direction, and in a moment, he saw four coyotes, running away from the approaching storm. His horse whinnied and turned his head to follow the coyotes. Not ten yards behind the coyotes, two jackrabbits, bounded along, seemingly chasing their natural predator. There was a gust of wind, and now the smell of smoke. A family of prairie dogs rumbled by circling wide around the horse and rider. As he watched the prairie dogs race away, he saw that his trailing horse had broken free and was running from the approaching storm.

When he turned his head back, he now saw a line of fire across the ground moving in his direction. The wind was now stronger and the smoke had intensified. The realization hit; a lightning bolt must have started a prairie fire. It was blowing his way. The animals were fleeing from the fire. The line of flames devoured the dry prairie grass and now spread across the horizon growing in size and, intensity. A flock of blackbirds raced overhead. His horse stamped and twisted again attempting to follow the other animals.

The wind now gusted. Sparks and firebrands blew past and the smoke thickened. The horse snorted in fear. The wall of flames threatened menacingly, its heat now being felt. Movement overhead grabbed Douglas' attention. Coming over the blowing smoke, Douglas saw a dark line of heavy clouds that stretched in a broad arch from the north to the south horizon, rolling overhead. Dampness filled the air. The clouds looked like a thick black shelf darkening the western sky and consuming the light overhead. Lightning flashed and thunder boomed.

A floating firebrand splashed on against them, and Douglas' horse let out a human-like squeal and bolted. Douglas held on and let the frightened animal run. After nearly a quarter-mile at a hard gallop, the horse began tiring. They had moved some distance from the prairie fire and the weather front. Douglas saw a dry wash and turned the horse into it, heading towards a lower elevation. It soon became a dry creek bed, and they stopped to rest under a sandstone overhang where flowing water had washed away the soil as it flowed to lower elevations.

Running Horse with his captive and Little Bear continued their trek in a direction that would lead them back towards the Comanche homeland. As the storm with its line of dark clouds approached, the warriors took shelter in a small cave along the Brazos River. Outside, the storm spirits sent forth the Thunder Bird in a show of anger; the wind blew dark clouds across the sky, lightning flashed and the sky's rumbled. Running Horse looked at his companion, and then at his captive and smiled arrogantly.

"Little Bear, you have nothing to show from our scout, but one weapon," chided Running Horse in his native tongue. "I bring a prize to camp, the yellow-haired woman. Perhaps you can use that rifle to bring us a deer."

As a challenge to his companion, Little Bear walked over towards Anna who sat curled on the ground, with her knees protectively in front of her. Using the rifle barrel, he lifted the torn dress slightly revealing the woman's scratched and bloodied feet and legs; he grinned wickedly.

Anna pulled away and pulled her dress back down. "My husband will track you, and kill you!" she spat.

"Husband is fool. He die," Running Horse snarled in his guttural English. To his companion, he gestured with his knife towards the cave opening and said in Comanche tongue, "Prove you are a man, kill a deer, or bring back a scalp."

Douglas had dismounted and left his horse in the dry creek bed. He climbed out of the gully and looked into the blowing wind to check the progress of the storm and the line of flames. The wind gusted harder full of sparks, skies darkened as the cloud line passed directly overhead, and the wall of flames bore down, only a hundred yards away. Suddenly, large drops of water splashed in his face; rain began falling, blowing really, stinging his exposed face and hands. The flames continued, closer, their heat searing. Now he was soaked by the cold rain; the flames sizzled like bacon, the moisture now dueling with the blowing firebrands. He was choked by the thick smoke.

Suddenly, Douglas felt a tremendous dread, fearing for the safety of Anna. Her sweet face flashed in his memory. Did she escape the hell that was the fire? Was she in this storm, drenched and cold? Was she still a captive? Or was she lost in the fire and wind storm somewhere on the prairie?

The flames were nearly upon him, persisting in spite of the rain. Douglas turned to step down into the gully and hide in the sandstone cavity created by

Hell and High Water

flowing waters turning to find lower ground. His feet slid in the slippery mud, and he fell tumbling into more wet mud and a puddle down below where moments before had been dry sandy soil.

Douglas coughed and spat mud and water; he raised his face from the puddle he lay in. Had he been unconscious? He didn't know, but now he was cold and wet; water rushed beneath as he rose to his hands and knees. Rain gushed down, freezing cold, like the time he had stood under a waterfall. Suddenly, there was a low rumble, not from the sky overhead, but seeming to come from up the hill where a stream of water rushed past his feet and flowed in the swale down to a lower portion of the prairie.

The rumble was suddenly louder, like a boat ride entering the rapids on a river. Douglas looked up, as a wall of water crashed down upon him sweeping him off his feet, and pulling him along like a leaf in a stream. Banged and bumped by hidden rocks and tree branches, he struggled to keep his head above water, to breathe. A mile or two later, exhausted, he was able to grab onto a branch of a willow tree that lay across the fast-flowing stream. Spent, he pulled his body onto the trunk of the fallen tree, gasping to catch his breath, and then he slowly shimmied along the tree back towards solid ground, and lay there, exhausted.

Douglas awoke wet, cold, and shivering still draped over the fallen tree. In the dim light from the graying sky, he saw a trickle of water flowing down the creek bed along with a scattering of branches and debris deposited by the flash flood. A distant burnt smell lingered, but the prairie grass here was matted and bent from wind and water, yet unburned. He heard a plaintive cry and the sound of struggle and splashing water. Instinctively, he rolled off the fallen tree and hid. In a few moments, the cry and struggle were heard again, downstream in the willow thicket. Cautiously, Douglas crawled over the wet ground towards the sound. There he saw a horse, apparently stuck amid downed and broken tree branches, unable to free itself.

Upon closer look, it was a Palouse, a spotted native pony. He stayed hidden, fearful of a trap. After some time, he edged closer and saw that the animal's hind leg was pinned between two loose branches that had wedged together in the water flow. As he approached, the pony snorted and shied away, fearful of the white man's scent. He spoke softly, and gently stroked the animal's wet fur on the shoulder and slowly towards the hindquarters and thigh, checking for injury. The pony settled and stopped its struggle. Douglas carefully lifted and separated the branches that pinned the leg, he then took the rawhide war bridle and guided the pony back slowly until it was freed.

As he led the Palouse out of the water, Douglas saw an Native warrior lying unconscious near the water's edge about 50 yards downstream. As he tied the pony's bridle to a tree branch, he realized that he had no weapons; all had been lost in the storm. Quietly, he circled around to get closer and found a thick branch to use as a club. As he snuck closer, he observed that the warrior appeared to have drowned in the flood. He was a short stocky man, and next to him lay a flintlock rifle. It was his Kentucky Rifle! This must be the warrior who took Anna!

Douglas searched the stream bed looking desperately for Anna. Then he remembered, he had been following two sets to tracks, two ponies, one riding double. Anna must still be out there, somewhere. He found the warrior's knife, took his rifle, and wiped it free of debris and mud, and then led the Palouse pony back upstream, looking for tracks left by the warrior and his pony. The Palouse seemed to want to pull away from the stream and head northwest; so, Douglas mounted the pony and let the animal follow its instinct for going home.

When the storm had passed, Running Horse walked in a circle near the cave opening, and in a few moments, he returned with a handful of small red berries. He ate a handful full and a few dropped near Anna. Running Horse then led his pony to some nearby grass and let the animal nibble on the plants and drink from a puddle. Anna was starved but said nothing. As her captor stepped out with the pony, she quickly grabbed the berries left by her feet and stuffed them in her mouth.

"Eww. These are awful!" Her words surprised her.

Hell and High Water

"Eat. Now ride, " said Running Horse in his guttural English. He then put Anna onto his pony and mounted behind her. They set off onto the prairies again. By dusk, they had reached the Comanche camp. Dogs barked in excitement; mothers and children collected in small groups to watch as Running Horse rode through the camp proudly, displaying his captive. A few old men appeared and nodded approvingly. Running Horse stopped briefly at the lodge of elder, Great Elk, to display his prize from the scout.

He then circled the village and made his way back to his own lodge where wife Little Flower stood at the entrance holding his infant son as the baby nursed at her breast.

"What is this?" Little Flower barked in her native tongue. "You go to bring us meat, yet you return with this scrawny yellow-haired dog."

"I bring you a slave-" he replied firmly, as he pushed Anna from the horse, causing her to fall to the ground between them. "-to carry wood, fetch water, and skin meat, while you care for our little one."

Other women had gathered around and began taunting Anna, as she fearfully hunched on her hands and knees.

The Palouse stepped carefully at its own pace, wending its way in a northwesterly direction. The land was charred, and it smelled of dampness mixed with the smoky odor of burnt remains. Suddenly, they crossed the fire line, into unblemished prairie grass. Douglas let the horse take its own lead, figuring it knew the way to its homeland. Anna's smiling face drifted into his consciousness, with memories of her soft touch, her warmth, and intimate closeness from their bed, providing a brief reprieve from the urgency of his purpose. The momentary glow of warmth was followed quickly with an immense sense of loss, a fear that he was too late, that deathly harm had already befallen his dear wife.

The Palouse maintained an even pace throughout the day, passing signs of wildlife on this seemingly barren plain. A large bird, which looked to be an eagle, circled overhead and then floated away in the upper air currents. The Palouse carefully stepped through a prairie dog village, with burrowed holes and small dirt mounds, spread over several acres. Later, trampled ground showed that a buffalo heard had moved north recently. Twice the Palouse had found a small stream where they paused to drink and rest. Despite his anger for the capture of his wife, Douglas felt respect for the Comanche's ability to live and survive on the open plains.

A dog barked, and a woman's voice called out; Douglas warmly recalled his visit to have dinner with Anna's family at their Tennessee mountain cabin when they began courting. The Palouse broke stride and lurched as it stepped over a small ravine. Douglas shook his head, he had been dozing, dreaming while on the pony. Was it really a dream? Another dog bark, women's voices, and the sounds of horses alerted Douglas that he was near a village. Could it be the Comanche village? He tugged at the bridle and pulled the pony into cover behind some sagebrush. The pony resisted, showing its desire to join the herd. This must be the Comanches.

The sun's orange glow faded in the west as he tied the Palouse and snuck closer on all fours to observe, anxiously hoping to see wife Anna somewhere in the village. He saw about twenty lodges, and a herd of ponies was gathered on the north edge of the camp. The lodges were cone-shaped tent-like shelters of buffalo hide wrapped around tall poles, with an entry opening on one side. There were three or four campfires, where women were preparing food and watching children.

Near one lodge, men congregated, talking and laughing, their actions sometimes punctuated with wild gestures demonstrating their actions. A dog barked, and a second chimed in. Douglas put his finger in his mouth and held it up to test the wind direction. Keeping crouched and low, he rotated around the camp to remain downwind, so that the animals would not be spooked by his presence. He could hear voices in the 200-yard distance; while he did not understand the words, the tone and inflection of voices revealed the emotions of the speakers. They seemed to be a happy people despite their hard nomadic life.

Suddenly, there was a piercing scream, a girl's scream, and all stopped to look and listen. Was that Anna? There was movement and a group of women congregated near a campfire in the corner by the ponies. Douglas heard more

Hell and High Water

screaming, and then laughter. There was a flash of movement between two lodges, yelling and taunting, and then a flurry of movement of yellow hair, in the midst of others with dark hair. Anna! It had to be Anna, screaming, and fighting! Instinctively he started to run towards her, but stumbled on a rock and fell. Douglas lay there, coming to his senses. "I can't run into that village now. It would be suicide. I have to think, I have to rescue her tonight, when they are sleeping," he thought.

It took forever for Comanches to go to sleep. Even though he shivered in the cool night air, Douglas struggled to stay awake. Finally, fires faded, the women and children slept, and the warriors drifted back to their lodges. Quiet settled on the village, interrupted briefly by a distant coyote. Walking cautiously, leading the Palouse, he made his way towards the village, circling around to the area where he had last seen the women tormenting Anna. He left the pony to join the herd, and slowly edged towards the lodges, listening, looking for some sign.

He froze when he saw an animal tethered to a stake and curled in a ball outside the pointed shelter. The furry ball stirred and made a soft crying sound. There was more movement, revealing a bloodied foot, and a moan, and then light-colored hair emerged. Anna! It had to be Anna, tied up outside like a dog, covered in a small animal skin.

"Anna," he whispered, touching her shoulder.

"Aaahh!" Anna gasped in fear, trembling at the surprise touch.

"Shh, it's me, Douglas, I'm getting you out of here."

Her hands covered her face and she shivered in fear. Then her eyes blinked open. "Dougie, …I knew you would come." Weakly, her hands opened up to him.

There was a sound of a cough and mumbled grunt from inside the buffalo skin lodge. Douglas quickly produced a knife and cut the rawhide that bound Anna's leg to the stake. Whispering in her ear, he picked her up and carried her towards the herd of ponies, looking for the Palouse that had led him to the camp.

But, where had it gone? The herd was a mass of spotted ponies. In the dark they all looked alike. The ponies snorted and stomped, backing away from the two strange smelling white people who stumbled into their midst. Nearby, a dog barked, sounding an alarm mirrored by the ponies.

Now he heard voices, men's voices, calling out an alarm. Finally, Douglas found the familiar Palouse, placed Anna on the pony, and leaped up behind her, turning the animal and kicking its sides to break away.

The pony was fleet, a good runner, and now responsive to his leads. In the darkness, he sensed a gully and tugged on the pony's mane to head down into the trough to better hide their retreat. Behind, he heard the yells and excitement as the village came alive and went to the horses in pursuit. The darkness helped to cover their escape, but it offered little advantage. Riding double would slow their escape. Douglas knew that the Comanches were excellent horsemen, able to track and read sign like a preacher reads the Bible.

They rode hard trying to gain some distance from the village. After a bit, the Palouse tugged to the left and slowed as the prairie gave way to a gully. Douglas now smelled the dampness of a pond or stream. He let the pony lead to water. When the animal's hooves splashed into the stream, he dismounted, and helped his wife; they all rested and drank thirstily. Douglas listened, and for the moment at least, he did not hear the Comanches. Then he scanned the starry sky and recognized the three stars of Orion's belt in the southern sky. When they resumed, he pointed the Palouse just left of that direction. Knowing that there were miles to cover, he nudged the Palouse to an easy canter. Soon, with the rocking motion of the pony, Anna seemed to nod off with her head on his shoulder.

The Palouse had slowed to a walk, tired from the night's journey. A touch of gray peeked from the eastern horizon. There was a whistle from a nearby ridge ahead, a two-toned trill that Douglas recognized as a bobwhite quail. Then, he heard a second trill to his right, and the Palouse's ears flicked, in each direction. The Palouse turned to the right, seemingly pulled towards the sound. Douglas felt a tingle in the hair on his neck; he pulled at the rein and kicked the Palouse's sides to urge it forward. A shadow of a man appeared on

Hell and High Water

a pony frozen like a statue. Then Douglas heard the twang of a bowstring, and an arrow found its mark in Douglas's right arm.

Douglas groaned in pain and Anna squealed in fear, as the Palouse lunged forward. Another arrow flew just inches from their faces. Two shots boomed from just ahead. Douglas feared that they were heading further into a trap and he turned the Palouse, seeking an escape route. His eyes caught movement to the rear where he saw a Comanche warrior limping away to the cover of a ravine. From the left, there came the sound of galloping hooves, then a gunshot.

Douglas turned his head quickly, fearing death by a Comanche warrior. To his surprise, he saw Ranger Jake, riding hard, Colt in hand, flushing one last Comanche from hiding. Moments later, Jake returned.

"You're a sight for sore eyes," said Douglas. "I feel like we've been through hell and high water. How did you know where to find us?"

"Had a report of Comanches in the area, and stopped by your place to check on ya," replied Jake. "Saw the tracks in your yard. Told the story, Miss Anna been taken and you went after her. Then the storm hit, washing away the trail. But, I knew they'd head back to the Comancheria; I've tracked them up this way before."

"We're mighty appreciative," said Anna. As she turned to look at her husband, she saw the arrow through the muscle of her husband's arm. "Oh my! Douglas, you're hurt. We've got to take care of that!"

Douglas grimaced and nudged the Palouse. "Enough of this palaver, we gotta get some miles between us and those Comanches before they regroup for another try."

Holding a steady pace and watching their back trail, the trio covered ground most of the day. Late afternoon, they stopped briefly to rest the horses, remove the arrow from Douglas' arm, and to bandage the wound. They made it back to the Austin area by noon, the following day.

"You saved our lives, Ranger Jake," said Anna, after they arrived back at the ranch. "Now I insist that you accept our thanks by staying for dinner."

"Yes'm. I'd be mighty obliged." Jake smiled sheepishly, removing his hat as he stepped into their mud log home. "I hear tell you're a mighty fine cook, ma'am."

# #

Spirit Warrior

Can a drifter and a Native woman with child survive on the trail?

The midday sun glared down with such intensity that Thomas McCord's own shadow hid surreptitiously under his feet. Reins were tied loosely around his wrist to prevent accidental dropping as he led his tired horse across the dusty expanse of the New Mexico desert. Each shuffle of his feet kicked up small dust clouds. A drop of sweat dribbled from his hatband down his neck, and on down his back. In the distance, the mountains shimmered like dark spikes waving in a non-existent breeze. Midway, a round shiny lake glistened.

"Damn Mirage!" The words came from dry lips and a swollen tongue. The Dun snorted in reply.

Thomas had been tracking west on the Santa Fe Trail in 1840. In his 26 years, he had been a trapper, hunter, Indian fighter, and now a drifter. At the Canadian River ford, the stream had been reduced to a muddy trickle, hardly enough to slake the thirst of man or beast. His canteen was nearly dry again. He'd been walking, leading his animal for the past two days due to the unremitting heat. Common sense argued for night travel to avoid heat and Comanches. But, cloudy skies, too dry to give up rain, blocked views of the stars eliminating any chance of night-time navigation on an unfamiliar trail. A Hawken rifle hung on a boot attached to his saddle and two percussion pistols were strapped to his belt for a quick pull in the event of hostiles.

There was a buzz by his ears, and Thomas turned to see two bees buzzing in a westerly direction. He paused momentarily, looking at the southwestern direction of the trail, and then sighting on a distant butte rock in line with the bees travel direction. *Bees,... flowers,... water.* He turned westerly, aiming towards the distant butte. After what he guessed to be an hour, he came across carcass remains of a dead animal, looked to be a mule, stripped of any valuables and its flesh mauled by predators. A mile or two later, still sited towards the distant butte rock, two vultures circled lazily.

"'Nother dying body, mebbie walked away from the mule," he observed, thinking *funny how on these long lonely journeys, you tend to talk to yourself, or your animal.* The Dun snorted and pulled back on the reins, perhaps catching the drifting smell of death that had attracted the predators circling overhead. Thomas reassuringly touched the pistol at his waist and pressed on. *Nothing of value with the mule, but there might be bootie up ahead.*

There was a high-pitched cry and he turned quickly to his left, pulling a pistol from his belt. Scanning the horizon near and far, only barren dry desert was revealed. After a few cautious steps over a rise, the squeaky noise repeated. His eyes zoomed towards a boulder sitting in the center of a dry creek bed. He dropped the reins and pulled the Hawken from the saddle boot. Stealthily, he began to circle towards the boulder, weapon cocked and ready to fire. The squeaky sound repeated, louder this time. *A Comanche warrior? No. He'd have just killed me. Animal? Maybe. Baby animal? Possibly.* As he approached, he saw a tiny cubby hole under the boulder, maybe an animal den. As he neared, he pulled a knife from its sheath. He pounced, knifepoint first, ready to do battle with bobcat or coyote or another sharp-toothed creature.

"Ayeeia!"

"Wyaaa! Wyaaa! Wyaaaaa."

"Wha? A baby!" Thomas fell back on his butt, away from the cubby, shocked that he had nearly stabbed a copper skinned human baby.

"¡Irse! Go away!" It was a Hopi girl, speaking a mix of Spanish and her native Hopi dialect. She crawled out slowly, untangling arms and legs from that tiny dark hole, cradling her baby. Dusty and dirty with scraggly black hair and fear in her eyes, the girl held a tiny newborn baby in one hand and a broken, bloodied knife in the other, waving the knife in Thomas' direction.

Spirit Warrior

"Hold on! Hold on. I'm not going to hurt you or your baby." Thomas backed up, hands open, pointing the rifle up and away. "Water,....I have some water for you and the baby." He stepped to his horse, removed the canteen, and shaking it to show it contained water, handed it to the girl. Cautiously, she set the knife down, accepted the canteen, dabbed some water drops to the baby's lips, and took a small drink.

Thomas observed that the baby was a newborn, less than a month old. The mother, a girl really, looked to be maybe 15 or 16 years of age. She wore a beaded leather dress, once pretty, but now stained with blood and dirt. Matted black hair hung down to her delicate shoulders. She knew only a few words in Spanish and spoke her native Hopi dialect.

Since Thomas did not speak any Native dialects, they finally reverted to hand gestures and signs to communicate. After some effort, Thomas learned that her warrior husband had died in battle and she was returning to her people, the Hopi, when a white man had stolen her horse. She was called Catori because she was sensitive to the spirits.

The temperature moderated as the sun descended in the western sky, soon dropping below the mountains on the horizon. Thomas helped Catori and her baby up onto the Dun, and he led them westerly as Catori directed. They rested during the coldest hours of the night and were traveling again as the skies grayed in the east.

"¡Mira! Look!" Catori pointed to the sky, ahead. Two turkey vultures lazily circled, maybe a mile away. Thomas pulled the Hawken from its boot and checked its load. They proceeded cautiously. As they neared, Thomas observed a form on the ground, a man, dying or dead. The large black bird had landed and picked at the body, then hopped back in response to what appeared to be a weak swat. The bird pranced in small circles, approaching the body again, anticipating its next meal. Thomas picked up a stone and threw it, causing the predator to squawk angrily and lunge skyward in retreat.

"El malo, The bad one," said Catori as she made a sign depicting how the man had attacked her and taken her horse. She showed Thomas where her knife blade had cut the thief in defense of her life. Up close now, the man clearly was dead. The man's clothes were torn and dusty, his body streaked with open cuts about the face and hands, which were caked with a mixture of dirt and dried blood. The eyes openly glared skyward and the mouth was frozen in an "Oh" of fear. Speckles of ants were seen on the skin and garments.

Catori circled around his body cautiously, keeping her distance, shielding her baby from the dirty corpse. She spoke again, with gestures, "espíritu matarlo, the spirit killed him."

"Whaa,…what do you mean?"

"Espíritu matarlo, the spirit killed him," she repeated, again with gestures, pointing to a trail of running footsteps, a fall, and then drag marks ending in a puddle of dried blood. She kicked dirt onto his face and smiled triumphantly as if a wrong had been righted.

"You ain't gonna need these anymore." Thomas picked up a gun from the man's belt, and unstrapped an ammunition pack, pulling it away from the body. He shook the ants off. A shadow flashed on the ground, and Thomas glanced up squinting at the glaring sun as the vulture circled overhead.

"Wyaaa! Wyaaa!"

"Agua allí. Water there," said Catori as she pointed in the direction of the thief's footprints. They followed the footsteps in the sandy soil down a dip of a dry wash that flowed to a gully, and then to a crack in the ground. Nearby a stub of what looked to be a lone cottonwood tree clung to the side of the gully. All around the ground looked bone dry. Thomas's hopes sank as their feet kicked up small clouds of dust.

"Wyaaa! Wyaaa!"

"Rare….rare….cluck." It was a scratchy sound, Thomas turned towards the barren tree and saw a plump iridescent black bird, with a thick beak sitting on a branch. It was a raven. He turned to look at the dry crack in the ground, hoping to see some dampness.

"Oh!" The girl's voice sounded frightened, surprised. Then there was a quiet cooing from the baby. Thomas turned around and was taken aback. There, next to the tree, stood an ancient Native warrior, dark rust-colored skin all mottled and aged by the wind and sun. Wearing only a deerskin breechclout and moccasins, with two black feathers tied in his thick mane of silver hair, he appeared to be a man of great strength, capable of great feats, yet still projecting an aura of peace and tranquility.

"Cheveyo, the Spirit Warrior," whispered Catori. She knelt before the ancient warrior, her voice quietly whimpering, supplicating herself and holding her child up as a blessing to this venerable being. The child continued to coo softly as the old man accepted the child into his arms. The ancient one's lips moved silently, smiling upon the infant whose small hands reached out to touch the aged face.

In his mind, Thomas felt the strength and peace of this being and now feeling unafraid by the ancient one's sudden presence; somehow, he knew instinctively that the man standing before him to be a warrior spirit. The ancient one then held the child up facing East, and hummed a mysterious chant, then turned successively to the South, then West and finally to the North before returning the child to its mother.

The ancient one's firm countenance and obsidian eyes bore through Thomas *"Traveler, you have demonstrated a good heart by helping a mother and her child in their time of need. Your selfless concern for others is recognized by the spirits, and shall be rewarded."*

Thomas understood the thoughts, though no words were spoken. *"Others, whose heart is evil reap what they sow, and the spirits deliver due retribution for their self-serving ways."* As these thoughts were conveyed to Thomas, his mind pictured the ghastly fear registered on the face of the dead thief who lay a few short yards away.

The intensity of feeling from this unspoken communication caused Thomas to glance back towards where the thief's body lay. When his eyes returned, he saw only Catori and the baby. She was now kneeling near the crack in the earth as a small seep bubbled forth providing a cold wet source of life-giving water. He quickly looked around, but the ancient one was gone. Thomas' senses heard silence, broken only by the gurgling sounds of bubbling water and a nursing infant. They rested there for the night, Thomas sharing with Catori some dried bacon strips and flatbread from his saddlebag. The baby nursed, burped, and then slept in his mother's arms.

The air chilled and a million stars speckled the night sky. Somewhere a distant coyote howled to the slim crescent moon. Later, as the moon slid on its westward journey overhead, Thomas heard sounds- growling, squawks, and flapping of wings- sounds of a tussle in the darkness that drifted across the desert as nature's predators quarreled over their prize. His sleep was fitful, with images of death and then dreams of talking birds, and milky apparitions rising from the ground to the sky.

They moved out early the next day, heading southwesterly looking to meet the trail to Santa Fe. Thomas walked, leading his horse as Catori and the baby rode. The temperatures rose with the sun, it's blistering heat baking exposed skin and causing beads of sweat to drip from head and hair. A few times the baby fussed, but Catori quieted him quickly.

"¡Mira allí! Look there!" Catori pointed forward to dust rising on the trail ahead. The waviness of heat rising from the desert looked like a blur to Thomas. After a few moments, she added, "Comancheros, los malos. Comancheros, the bad ones."

Thomas reached for the Hawken, pulling it from the boot by the saddle. He had heard about the Comancheros, Mexican traders who bought and sold goods between the Mexicans, Natives, and Whites. But, many of the Comancheros were not just merchants, rather, they had a reputation of being brutal thieves, stealing goods from one to sell to another at a profit. Because of their brutality, he feared for the safety of Catori and the baby. He checked his loads.

As they approached, he saw three on horseback and one leading a small two-wheeled wagon, its goods covered by a tarp. The Comancheros stopped, blocking the roadway, about 100 feet in front of Thomas and Catori.

"What have we here?" He appeared to be the leader, heavyset, unshaven, a mouth of yellowed and missing teeth and an evil grin, with his eyes fixed on the young beautiful Catori and her baby.

"Mighty fine. Fetch a nice price," said the skinny one sitting atop the wagon, as he licked his lips, his mouth already salivating. The horse snorted and shook his head.

"Not buyin',... not sellin'," said Thomas, the strength of his voice surprising him. Thomas stood his ground, the Hawken cradled in his elbow pointing slightly forward but not directly at the threatening men before him. "Kindly step aside, we're traveling to Santa Fe."

"Mighty fine. I saw her first," said the skinny one, licking his lips. He pulled a pistol from his belt.

"Don't even think about it," growled Thomas as he swung the Hawken directly at the man's chest. He let the reins drop from his right hand as his fingers wrapped around the trigger. "Hammer's already set. Won't miss this close. Blow your head off,..." He let the Hawken swing slowly to each man's chest so that they could look down the gaping dark 50 caliber barrel.

The heavyset man's horse snorted nervously and twisted its head, sidestepping, sensing the tension. The man jerked the reins tightly. Just then a black flash swooped by right in front of the Comancheros' horses, looked to be a large black raven, causing the three animals to jump up and back.

BOOM!

Thomas fired the Hawken knocking the fat leader from his horse, and he quickly dropped the rifle and reached to his belt for the pistol. He felt the Dun bolt as Catori urged the mount sideways, away from the tormentors. The Dun's hip nudged Thomas sideways, causing a shot fired by the skinny one to miss its mark. Thomas leveled his pistol and fired, causing a jolt and look of surprise on the face of the skinny one sitting on the wagon.

The other two Comancheros fought to control their mounts, one falling underfoot. Thomas glanced sideways seeing Catori, clearly an accomplished rider, guide the Dun swiftly using only his mane into the desert and down into a dry wash putting distance and cover between herself and the attackers. Thomas fired at the third horseman, seeing his bullet score as the man screamed and spun from his still stumbling animal. The fourth man was slowly getting to his feet, as Thomas pulled a Bowie style knife from his boot and lunged at the man.

They grappled, grunted, gouged, and rolled in the dirt. Though shorter than Thomas, the man was stocky and strong, their hands locked together, as

Thomas tried to drive the knife into the man's throat. They tussled and rolled, it was a fight to the death. Then the man's knee came up and kicked Thomas in the gut knocking the wind out of him and pushing him away. Thomas rolled and came up staggering to his feet, now staring at the barrel of the man's pistol.

This is it, Thomas thought. *At least Catori and the baby have a chance to get away.* The raven buzzed in front of the man, screeching, wings flapping. The startled man stepped back, holding his hands up to protect his face pointing his pistol skyward. Thomas threw the knife hard, stabbing the man in the stomach, causing a look of surprise. The man looked down at the knife in his stomach to the hilt and slowly reached to pull at it. Blood dribbled from his lips, his color turned to a gray pallor and his eyes glazed over, knees crumbling and then he fell to his face.

Catching his breath, Thomas kicked the gun away from the man's hand, shoved him over with his boot, and pulled his knife from the man's bloody midsection. In the distance, he thought he saw the black bird flying over the desert, and then just below, he saw Catori, holding the baby, guide the Dun to a small rise, and turn to look in his direction. Thomas waved to her signaling that he was ok.

Later that day, as the sun glowed from the western horizon, Thomas and Catori rode into Santa Fe, leading the other two horses and the wagon.

"Four Comancheros attacked us, we defended ourselves Thomas explained to the Padre.

"Cheveyo – Spirit Warrior, save baby," said Catori to the Padre. "Cheyevo grandfather," she added proudly.

They left the goods with the padre at the mission as a donation to the church, with instructions on where to find the bodies for a proper burial. Thomas rode with Catori leading the horses to the nearby Hopi village back in the buttes. Catori and her baby were welcomed back by her family and the village elders. The horses were considered to be a gift by the gods to Catori's family for her perseverance in returning home after the loss of her husband in battle. While not understanding the words, Thomas clearly felt the appreciation and thanks of Catori's family for his role in her safe return.

Spirit Warrior

As he sat by the campfire, watching the reunited family, he remembered the words of Cheveyo, "Your selfless concern for others is recognized by the gods, and shall be rewarded. Others, whose heart is evil reap what they sow, and the gods deliver due retribution for their self-serving ways."

##

Kokopelli's Serenade

Does the spirit of Kokopelli foretell of new love or mischief?

"Muchas Gracias. Thank you so much, Estevan. The horse, she is a fine mare, sorely needed for the work on my land." Renaldo Rodriguez nodded and bowed slightly, his hands together in a submissive prayerful gesture as he spoke in his native Mexican language. "I am so grateful. How can I ever repay you for such a generous gift?"

"El gusto es mio, the pleasure is mine," replied Estevan, as he stood ramrod straight, a 22-year-old caballero decked out in a tailored charro suit and knee-high riding boots, holding his broad-brimmed high crowned sombrero in hand. "Please consider my proposal to you, for the benefit of our families. Your lovely daughter, Maria, is certainly most worthy to be considered as my bride. We will talk again soon." Estevan bowed at the waist, gallantly holding his sombrero out to the side.

A lovely 18-year-old, Maria stood silently at the doorway of the second room of the small two-room adobe mud block house, listening to the conversation between Estevan and her father. Estevan stepped towards her and took her hand, leading her out of the door into the dusty yard that surrounded the small house on their rancho on the outskirts of Santa Fe.

"Ouch! You are hurting me. Do not squeeze my hand so tightly."

Kokopelli's Serenade

"I fear that you wish to run away, that you do not wish to be my bride. There are many others who desire the honor that I offer to you. You are foolish to resist me. You will learn to love me."

"I am not sure. I need to think about this," said Maria as she pulled her hand out of Estevan's painful grip. "I wish my mother were still alive."

"You will learn to love me," he repeated, as he bowed, then turned and mounted his horse, and spurred it from the yard at a gallop, throwing dust and gravel into Maria's face.

"Tradition," she said to herself, "I hate it. He is mean and hurtful." A hand touched her shoulder. Maria turned and faced her father.

"I miss your mother, too. She believed in tradition. This caballero, he is from a fine family. Their large rancho is on a land grant from the governor. Estevan honors tradition. He brings gifts and he seeks your hand in marriage. You could do much worse."

Maria turned from her father and walked quickly into the house.

Clint Carrigan steered his freight wagon off the street and into an alley-way alongside *La Tienda* and set the brake. He needed to complete this last delivery of the day, to the general store, then he could collect his pay. Clint had signed on as a teamster in a wagon train hauling freight from Independence, Missouri to Santa Fe. It was 1840, and there were rumblings of war between the states and Mexico. As a result, merchants in Santa Fe began seeking alternative supply sources rather than rely on goods coming from south of the Rio Grande.

Clint anticipated a few weeks lay-over until a return trip would be scheduled to deliver furs and hides back to the east. The other teamsters had told stories about black-haired Mexican beauties and strong whiskey, and he was anxious to explore the town. He stood at the doorway of *La Tienda* and surveyed the street, locating the cantina where several horses were tied in front, a small church, the stable, a blacksmith shop, and a scattering of short adobe dwellings with small yards that he took to be homes of the local residents. In front of the little church, an old man wrapped in a serape sat cross-legged on the ground under a scraggly mesquite bush.

"Perdoneme, senior. Pardon me, sir."

Clint felt a slight nudge on the back of his arm, and he jumped a step forward, looking over his shoulder, as a petite young woman brushed quickly by, her eyes focused down to the ground as she walked quickly away. A wisp of an enticing floral aroma hung in the air momentarily and was gone as quickly as the petite girl.

His mouth opened to call out to the girl, but only a gasp was heard, the words stuck in his throat, overwhelmed by the fleeting glance of this dark-haired beauty. He felt his cheeks flush and quickly looked around to see if others were watching. But for the sleeping man in front of the church, the street was empty. Clint quickly went about his business, completing the delivery of goods to *La Tienda*.

The following week, Clint and fellow teamster Jake Owens were instructed to ride out to the canyons northwest of Santa Fe in search of wild mustangs to add to the shipping company's herd. It was mid-October, and there had been a morning chill in the air, but as the desert sun rose, so did the stifling heat. Small clouds of dust puffed with each step of the horses on the dry ground. They had not yet seen any sign of horses, and the heat seemed to drive away even the snakes and the desert horned lizards. In the distance, a mesa loomed. By mid-day, the dusty parched riders had reached the towering mesa and stopped to rest in the shade under an overhang of the vertical stone wall of the mesa. The absence of trees and bushes meant no twigs for a fire; the riders lunched on dried beef, flatbread, and a few sips of canteen water.

New to the area, Clint decided to explore and started to walk around the mesa. He rounded a corner, and then looked up in amazement, seeing the crumbled remains of what appeared to be small squared stone houses built into the mesa's vertical wall some fifty feet overhead. Searching further, he came upon a series of cut-out hand and footholds, that snaked up the wall towards the stone houses. He started climbing, but it was rough going because the wind and rain had worn down the edges of the footholds. Clint made it to a sheltered ledge, where he discovered some markings and pictures etched in the wall. One etching caught his attention, it appeared to be a man dancing while playing a horn or musical instrument. Clint returned to the shaded rest area and described his find to Jake.

"Where you been? We gotta get movin'. Boss wants us to come back with some horses."

"Hey, Jake, I found some houses up on the wall of the mesa. And, ...and there were markings carved in the stone. Pictures of critters and people!"

"Yeh, yeh. They say the Indians used to live up there. Ask Cheveyo, the spirit warrior."

"Who! What?"

"Cheveyo, the spirit warrior," said Jake impatiently. "He's the old Pueblo Native, sits in front of the church, wrapped in that serape. His people are the cliff dwellers who live in houses like those. He's crippled, can barely walk. The Padre found him nearly dead in the desert after a battle some years ago according to the old ones. Padre brought him back, and nursed him back to health. Cheveyo is blind, but somehow, he sees. He knows things, he hears things. Now, let's go get those horses."

The next day they picked up signs of unshod ponies, and followed the trail cautiously, unsure whether they followed a native war party or wild horses. Luck was with them; the trail led to a watering hole, surrounded by a small herd of wild ponies. Making use of a box canyon to corner the herd, Clint and Jake were able to sort a handful of strong healthy runners, to bring back to the teamster herd.

After a hard day, Clint slept soundly. During the night, he heard a musical sound, like a high-pitched flute, playing a happy song. Then, an image appeared. It was a dreamy misty image of the beautiful dark-haired girl who had passed him in front of *La Tienda*. A warm contented feeling settled about him. Who was this girl? He had to see her again. He would look for her upon his return to Santa Fe. Now awake, Clint looked up at a million sparkling stars in the black sky overhead. Such a strange dream thought Clint, a dream with music, and warmth, and feelings, like nothing he had ever experienced before. A shooting star streaked across the sky.

They returned to Santa Fe and delivered the herd of mustangs to the freight master. Clint saw Cheveyo again sitting in front of the church. Hesitantly, Clint walked past the old man who appeared to be sleeping.

"Meester Cleent. Come,…sit,…talk. You are hopeful, yet your mind is troubled with things you do not understand." The voice was deep and resonant, compelling Clint to stop, turn around and return to face the ancient one.

"How do you know my name,…and what I might be thinking?"

"Sit, Meester Cleent. You are new to Santa Fe, coming from the place where the sun rises. You are enchanted by a beautiful girl, yet humbled and words choke in your throat. And now you meet Kokopelli and hear his serenade. And so you seek the wisdom of Cheveyo."

"I have said nothing, how do you know these things of me?" Clint sat on a nearby tree stump.

"Kokopelli is a spirit of fertility and change. You have heard the happy song of his magical flute, you are being asked to create fertility in your life. I encourage you to heed his entreaty. But, beware of the challenge of other suitors. A worthy achievement comes only with much effort. Only the strongest cougar wins his desired mate. Now, go forth as your heart directs."

Then Cheveyo's head nodded under the serape and he remained silent. After a few moments of silence, Clint rose and silently walked away.

It was the end of October and the nights were getting chilly as winter's cold winds announced its impending arrival first in the higher elevations and then upon the lowlands. Clint awoke, cold, groggy, and hungover after a night of drinking with Jake in the cantina. He heard voices, laughter, gleeful screams of children, and music. As he stepped out to the street, he saw that the festivities were over at the church, near the adjoining graveyard. He walked to the cantina, where the enticing smells of coffee, eggs, and fried meat now filled the air, replacing the odors of whiskey and smoke from the night before. The bartender's wife greeted him.

Kokopelli's Serenade

"Buenos dias, amigo. ¿Qué le gustaría comer? Good morning, friend. What would you like to eat?"

"Huevos con carne y pan,… y café, por favor. Eggs with meat and bread, …and coffee, please. " In the weeks that he had been in Santa Fe, Clint was making an effort to learn the Spanish language which was the main language of the community under the rule of Mexico.

" What's happening at the church?"

"It is the day of the dead, a celebration to remember deceased loved ones."

Clint watched the festivities. It was a happy and colorful holiday. The young and old alike were visiting the cemetery, placing decorations on the graves, and spending time there - in the presence of their deceased friends and family members. Then, there was music and dancing. The festive beat of the music drew Clint closer, soon he was in the midst of the activities, stamping his foot to the beat. His arm was nudged from the rear and he turned around.

"Your feet tap to the beat of the music. Do you like to dance?"

It was the dark-haired girl, looking into his eyes, with a smile, and swaying to the beat of the music. Clint was momentarily breathless, but he caught himself, smiled, nodded his head, and said, "yes, I love to dance. Would you like to dance with me?"

"Yes, I would love to," she said with a glowing smile. "My name is Maria."

"I'm Clint,…Clint Carrigan." Soon they were spinning and swaying along with the other dancers. As he danced Clint savored the moment. Maria's golden olive complexion was radiant, her brown eyes sparkled, and her black hair shined in the sunlight, bouncing on her shoulders with the beat of her steps. Maria and Clint looked in each other's eyes and smiled. It felt like they were in a dream, the only two people dancing on a stage, as lights and faces spun around them.

Suddenly, there was a hard jolt, knocking Clint off the dance area. He stumbled and reached to keep Maria from falling. Then there was a hard kick in his rear, that separated his hold on Maria's hand and sending both of them onto the dusty ground followed by a gasp of shock, from the other dancers.

Clint rolled and spun, coming to his feet, as if thrown from a bucking horse, his legs now spread and arms rising in defense. There was a blur of motion and a scream from a nearby lady, and Clint found himself tangled with a man, punching, and gouging as they rolled on the ground. Clint found an opening, kicking his knee up between them and pushing away with his leg. Then they stood face to face.

"Estevan. How could you? How could you spoil this day?" Maria stood nearly between them, arms on her hips. He was about Clint's age, maybe an inch or two shorter, with thick black hair and a short trimmed mustache, but clearly a handsome man, dressed in the stylish charro suit and riding boots.

"You behave like a whore. You are to be my wife. Yet you come here and dance with strange men in front of others. You shame yourself. You shame me." His eyes were locked on to Clint, with a glare of hate as he spoke harsh words directed to Maria. "Go, you whore, while I take care of this,…this devil intruder."

After Maria had stormed off in a mix of shame and anger, Estevan stepped towards Clint, holding his hands in tight fists. "If you come near her again, I will kill you. It truly will be your day of the dead." He turned, picked up his sombrero, and dusted himself off. Then strutted over to his horse, leaped into the saddle, and spurred the horse at a gallop towards Clint. Clint jumped back away from the horse's path, as Estevan rode quickly away.

Winter came early to the mountains and northern plains, with colder than normal temperatures, harsh winds, and blowing accumulating snows. The freight master determined that a return shipment of furs and hides now would be too dangerous. The shipment would be delayed until spring. Clint was kept busy with local deliveries, and training the mustangs that he had rounded up. Occasionally, he would catch some odd jobs for other ranchers or families in and around Santa Fe. He stayed busy, and while he thought often of Maria and the wonderful dance they shared, he remained uncertain what action would be appropriate, after all, the man had said that he was engaged to Maria. Clint thought that, if Maria loved this man, he would respect her feelings.

Kokopelli's Serenade

It was nearly the start of spring, and the harsh winter was beginning to release its grip upon the area. The freight master told Clint to report to *La Tienda* the next day in the morning for local delivery. That night, Clint had a restless night with difficulty sleeping. During the night, he had a dream, Kokopelli appeared, dancing with his flute and the happy sounds of better things to come. The sounds of the flute were so real, that Clint awoke, and walked around the out-building behind the stable where he slept. Must be a dream,… my imagination, he thought and laid down to sleep again. Later, in another dream, the image of Maria appeared, smiling and dancing to the magical sounds of Kokopelli's flute.

The next day, Clint reported to La Tienda with his wagon, loaded the merchandise, and followed the directions to deliver the goods to a local rancher, one Renaldo Rodriguez. As Clint pulled the wagon on the Rodriguez property, he met rancher Rodriguez working on a gate that was falling from the hinges, causing the gate to remain open and stock to escape. Clint helped Rodriguez to repair the gate, then he unloaded and stored the merchandise. It was still early afternoon, and Clint offered to ride out with Rodriguez to round up the lost stock, a horse and two cows.

When they returned with the stock at dusk, Clint saw someone standing near the door of the small house where Rodriguez lived.

"Thank you so much, young man. So helpful, so kind. You help me repair the gate, store our supplies, and even help to round up the stray stock," said Rodriguez.

"My pleasure sir. It looks like your wife is waiting for you. I'd best be going. It's nearly dark," replied Clint.

"She is my daughter, Maria. Unfortunately, my wife has passed on. We were in town to celebrate her passing on the day of the dead when that Estevan started that awful fight. He comes from a prominent family, I thought he was a fine young man, but I was wrong."

As Rodriguez spoke and mentioned Maria by name, Clint's eyes flashed to the house for another look. She seemed so familiar, he thought. "I met your daughter that day, sir. She is a lovely lady. I wish only the best for both of you." Clint shook Rodriguez's hand and waved to Maria, who remained standing by the door. As he turned and left, he saw that Maria had returned the wave, and, from fifty yards away, he could feel the warmth of her smile.

After making deliveries the next day, Clint stopped into the cantina at the end of the day for a drink. There was excited talk among the men in the cantina.

"He's going to do it. He's going to take her today. Not even wait for a wedding, maybe do the wedding when he gets her down to their estate."

"But, there should be a wedding, it is tradition. The father, Senior Rodriguez must give her away."

"I tell you Estevan is not waiting. He was drunk. Very angry. He fears Rodriguez has rejected the gifts. His daughter, Maria, she loves another."

Moments later, a rider came racing down the street, stopping in front of the cantina. "Help. Help. Senior Rodriguez is hurt bad!"

Clint dropped his drink, and ran out to the street, seeing Rodriguez all bloodied, falling from a horse. Clint knelt next to Rodriguez. Rodriguez grimaced, and mumbled in pain, "I returned the horse to Estevan, but he got angry and beat me. Then he took Maria,…back to his rancho."

Clint mounted his horse and rode south, towards the estate of Estevan's family. As he rode into the desert, the wind blew and a musical sound seemed to fill his head, he thought he could once again hear Kokopelli's flute. A few miles south of Sante Fe, he could see riders on two horses up ahead. Then the riders stopped, and one appeared to have fallen from the horse. They appeared to be arguing and did not see his approach. Then the taller one struck the smaller one who fell to the ground. As he neared he could see that it was Estevan standing over Maria as she appeared to rise, but was slapped again.

"Do not hit a lady! If you want to fight, you fight me," yelled Clint. He dismounted and stood before them.

Upon seeing Clint, Estevan's face flushed with anger, and he ran towards Clint, screaming, "You die! You die!"

Kokopelli's Serenade

Clint had grappled with the other teamsters in contests of strength during the westward trip and had even survived a knife attack by a Comanche during a skirmish with hostiles. Clint instinctively sidestepped the charging Estevan, caught a swinging arm, and used the charging man's momentum to hurl him to the ground. They fought hard, hitting, kicking, punching, gouging, and tumbling to the ground. At first, they were evenly matched, but Clint's years of hard work on the trail and loading merchandise gave him greater stamina.

After 30 minutes of sustained fighting, both men were sweating and dirty from their blows and rolling on the ground. When his opponent gasped for breath, Clint found an opening for a one-two punch, first to Estevan's midsection, and then to the chin, knocking him out. Exhausted and bloodied, Clint hoisted Estevan over the Mexican's own saddle, tied the still unconscious man to the saddle, and slapped the horse to start it on a homeward journey.

Aching and sore, Clint and Maria rode back into Santa Fe. Arriving in front of the cantina, they found Rodriguez, sitting on a stool at the front door. He smiled upon seeing that his daughter was OK. Maria and her father embraced, and Rodriguez then winked at Clint and said, "Muchas Gracias. Thank you so much, Senior Clint. You have saved my daughter and brought her back unharmed. I am so grateful. How can I ever repay you for such a generous gift? Maria speaks of you often. If you wish the hand of my daughter in marriage, you have my blessing."

# #

[Read Blazing Guns on the Santa Fe Trail for more Clint Carrigan Adventures]

The Hunted

Deer hunters now become the hunted, will they survive?

The bright midday sun was softened by dappled fluffy clouds overhead. There was a buzz of excitement among the 65 souls heading west on the Santa Fe Trail as twenty-two wagons pulled out of Independence on that 15th of May, 1851. Never mind that departure was four hours late because the lead wagon broke an axle upon hitting a boulder during the initial line-up, or that two children had become temporarily lost after wandering away from the staging camp south of town; this was our day of destiny.

We were embarking on our great pilgrimage west to the promised land, the west, exotic Santa Fe. Families, farmers, tradesmen, and adventurers, all seeking a new life in the west, and yes, for some, continuing on to the gold-filled hills near Sutter's Mill in California.

My name is James, James St. Clair. We St. Clair's hailed from central Indiana, but it was getting too crowded there. The stories abounded of the lush open lands of the west where there's more space and fewer people. Pa drove our wagon, pulled by two oxen, following the trails west from Indiana to Independence, Ma and little sister Mary rode, while Pa, older brother Joshua and me walked. My feet and legs were sore at first, but I soon got in shape. In Independence, Joshua and I were able to pick up two of the new Sharps rifle, a single-shot breech-loading weapon that was easier and faster to load and shoot compared to the muzzle-loading muskets in common use.

The Hunted

In the first few days, the wagon train traveled about 15 miles a day. But after a heavy rain at the end of the first week, we were lucky to make 5 miles a day as the wagons and animals trudged through the mud and mire. Joshua and I participated in the various hunting expeditions looking for game for the evening dinner. We were quickly recognized for our skill with the Sharps, often able to bag deer or antelope. We eagerly sought the prize of finding a herd of bison, but luck eluded us.

The smaller animals seemed to be found more readily on the prairie, while tracking the larger game often led us to the small stands of forest and tree lines that trailed the creeks and rivers of the Kansas territory. Listening to the wagon master over the dinner fire, we gained tracking knowledge and learned to recognize the signs, tracks, and scat of the various plains wildlife. Late one afternoon, several miles out, Joshua shot a deer. As we came upon our kill, excited about our catch, we were surprised to find an arrow in the animal's chest. This was a sure sign of a native hunting party. We looked, but we didn't see any.

The wagon master had said that Kiowa still roamed the territories west of Kansas City. We had hoped to avoid crossing their path because they were easily angered when the hunting activities of passing wagon trains took their food supplies. Leery, we took turns standing watch while we butchered the deer for a return trip to the wagon train. It was late and soon became dark, a moonless night with a million stars overhead, yet too dangerous to travel, so we made camp by a nearby creek.

The next morning, I got the fire re-charged, put coffee on to boil, and deer meat on a skewer. It seemed strangely quiet. Joshua was waking and stretching, muscles stiff from sleeping on the ground, when I heard a grunt, and I figured that Joshua was just getting a kink out of his shoulder. But I turned and saw Joshua holding his chest, his face white as a ghost, with blood dripping from his fingers. He slowly looked down at his hand on his chest, and I saw an arrow between his fingers, sticking out of his chest, blood covering his hand, and pink bubbles forming at his lips.

He collapsed into my arms and I saw the arrow protruding from his back. I pulled him away from the fire and leaned him against a nearby tree. Then, I felt a sharp pain as an arrow cut my arm and slammed into the tree behind me.

"Kiowa...." Joshua spoke in a whisper, choked with blood making pink bubbles in his mouth. "Run,... save yourself..." Joshua's words had become hoarse. He grimaced as reached for his Sharps. "Run, James, run," he coughed. "I'll cover you."

Joshua checked the action and aimed the Sharps in the direction where the arrows are coming from. "Go!" he ordered, "Go!...Now!...."

It felt like a bad dream. I would awake and everything would be OK. Then, another arrow flew by my ear, and instinctively, I obeyed my older brother. I grabbed my Sharps and ammunition pack and ran back into the stand of trees away from the attacker. I heard a wild yell, like nothing I've ever heard, and then the click and boom of Joshua's rifle.

I began running as fast as I could. I glanced over my shoulder and saw a dark-skinned man, naked from the waist up, several feathers in his hair, face, and body painted with brilliant colors, bounding my way. A terrified panic consumed me, my legs churned, stumbling, tripping. Then, I felt an arrow hit the butt of my rifle knocking it from my hand. There were two, three, or more, and they're coming my way yelping excitedly.

I ducked behind a tree and reached around to grab my rifle. Then, I sprinted off in a low crouch, jumping over deadfall logs, slipping on the leaves, ducking under low branches changing directions every twenty or thirty feet, like a fleeing rabbit. Every time I changed to a new direction, I heard another yelp, like they were signaling my moves. As I heard the yelps, I sensed that they had spread out, and they were easily keeping up with me. Running through the trees, I was getting scratched. Twigs and low branches clawed at my face and hands. They seemed to be enjoying the chase. Yesterday, I was the hunter; now, I am the hunted.

I had my stride now, but then, I realized that I had lost all sense of direction, I didn't know which way was back to the wagon train. It seemed like the chase had been going on forever, but I realized it had only been 10 minutes or so. I wasn't tired, but my breathing was fast, almost uncontrolled, due to the rush to get away from the flying arrows and those three warriors. I knew I needed

The Hunted

to take charge of my senses, hold down the panic, and focus my m... didn't take control, I'd lose my life.

When facing the threat of imminent death, instincts take over. In my mind, I flashed back to one of Pa's hunting lessons, "Son," he said, "once the animal spots you, he has three choices…freeze,…flight,…or fight. It makes that decision by instinct in about a half a second." My mind flashed its decision. Somehow, I needed to add distance, or take them out, one by one. I could hear them back there, three of them, spread out and keeping pace with me. I scanned the terrain ahead as I ran.

The ground began to slope downward, likely towards a stream bed or maybe the river at the bottom of the decline. I angled downward, lengthening my stride, jumping over obstacles, ducking under branches. Soon, I saw a gully, off to the left, about 40 yards. I zigged right and then bound over a fallen tree trunk, and then crouched and scrambled back to the left over towards the gully. My plan was to get to the ditch and hide as they passed, or perhaps have an opportunity to take one out.

The gully was a dry wash, about 3 feet deep and 10 feet across, with brush on its rim. I scrambled on all fours back up the dry gully and then ducked into a washed-out cavity under a bush. I put the rifle barrel over the edge, but under the bush, and froze. My heart was pounding, my chest heaving, sucking in air. I tried hard to calm my breathing, to stay still and quiet. Immediately, coming down the hill I saw movement, the pursuer closest on my trail. I was amazed at how he silently yet quickly moved through the trees. He went past me, about 20 yards out, down the slope. Suddenly, he stopped, just past the fallen tree trunk, turned, and made his way cautiously toward the gully. How could he know I went this way?

I slowly adjusted the rifle and sight in his direction. I can see his movement down the hill as he crossed towards the gully. Holding my breath, I heard a drop of moisture hitting a leaf below me. I glanced down and saw a drop of blood on the leaf, blood from my shoulder wound where the arrow had nicked me in the camp. Maybe he saw my blood on the ground…damn… I thought. I've left a blood trail for him to follow me to this spot.

Cautiously, he stepped into the gully, looked down, and then turned up towards my direction. I stayed frozen, with the bare-chested warrior in my sites. There were some fifteen yards between us, filled with debris, branches, and limbs. Soundlessly, he stepped over the leaves and branches, coming in my direction. My heart pounded so loud I was sure he could hear it beat. His head lifted slightly...he must have seen me and notched his arrow. I squeezed the trigger, heard the click of the hammer, and felt the kick and boom of my shot. The man fell back, and in the distance, I heard the yelps of the other warriors farther down the hill.

I took off running up the gully. It was rugged and treacherous. Stumbling, I jumped out towards the uphill ground, finding a steep incline out away from the gully. There were thick underbrush and deadfall tree branches covering over slippery muddy soil from a ground seep, that caused me to use hands and feet to pull up from one spot to the next. I was breathing hard from the steep climb, slipping, and bumping my knees on broken logs and exposed rocks. I scrambled over a stone outcropping, onto a low plateau of prairie overlooking the creek bed below.

There were no trees on the prairie, so I could gain some distance, but soon the pursuers would be over the ledge as well and have a clear shot at me. To the left was the waving grasses of the prairie. I stayed close to the river-washed precipice, looking for a way down back into the cover of the trees. I heard my pursuer's excited voices, but they had not yet reached the top. Then, I saw a gouge, an opening in the ground where water collects and drops over the ridge. It was steep, dropping off sharply, nearly vertical, but it looked like my only escape. I slid feet first, landing hard on my butt, bumping down the trough, trying to guide my direction feet first, one hand on my rifle and the other trying to keep a balance. My butt and my heels and my elbows took the brunt of this downward slide on hard rock.

Midway down, there was a landing of sorts where the falling water collected and pooled before washing down to the lower level. I pushed myself into a small ledge in front of a rounded cavern cut into an exposed sandstone cliff. It was a small cave, cut by the downward flowing water over the years. I stood, bumping my head on the low overhang; there was only about 4 feet

The Hunted

clearance. Here, I would make my stand. I squatted down and held my position listening for my pursuers. My heart was pounding, and my breathing labored. I heard voices overhead on the plateau.

I quickly reload my rifle, to be ready for the next opportunity to fire. I hear excitement overhead like they've found my trail. I must have left some mark, or foot scraping, or blood drop. Some small stones trickle down the trough, one is coming down after me. When he gets down, I'm trapped in this cave, a trap of my own choosing. My only chance is surprise. My eyes quickly survey the cave again, but there's no escape. More stones trickle down the trough…my heart beats faster, he's just moments away. I move to the right, into a shadow, with a view of the edge of the trough, …more stones are tumble down…I check my rifle, pulling the hammer back to full cock and site the trough just above where the little stones tumble downward. I quickly feel my belt and locate my sheath knife,…I may need it if my shot misses its mark.

My mind flashes back to that final image of Joshua, an arrow through his body, blood dripping from his lips as he whispers to me to run. I think of Ma, and little sister Mary, and wonder if I'll ever see them again. If I die here, they'll never find me. I remember Pa, and his stern admonishment to be careful. They'll never forgive me for letting Joshua die at the hands of the Kiowa.

I notice sprinkles of sun trickle down to the landing. I see the movement of a shadow, but now he's soundless, the shadow moving slowly. I'm kneeling, frozen at the ready, rifle pointed at the trough. He must know I'm here…how can he know that I'm in this cave? There's a flash of movement, I fire and the rifle kicks, I feel a tug on my tunic and a sting as something sharp cuts into the side of my chest under my arm. I must have blinked, my ears ache from the boom of the rifle in this tiny cave.

I see movement coming at me,… the painted muscular warrior. Instinctively, I swing the rifle's stock outward, striking the warrior with the butt of the weapon, and give it a second jab pushing the warrior backward. His tremendous strength resists and then freezes my push, and we're locked in a struggle, each with a grip of the weapon, on a narrow ledge, my head just inches from hard stone. His eyes are cold and fierce, his breath and body odor are putrid, nearly gagging me. I feel beads of sweat from my forehead and temples sliding down to my eyes.

My muscles begin to quiver, his strength is overpowering. He pushes me back and my head bumps the hard stone overhang behind me. Instinctively my head comes down and forward, in that moment I see blood oozing from his stomach. My bullet must have found its mark. With renewed vigor, I continue the motion slamming my head down onto his nose and mouth, as my foot finds the stone wall. I hear a crack of broken cartilage in the nose. I push hard drawing leg strength against the wall to push the warrior backward to a steep drop-off from the narrow ledge. His foot slips, I swing the rifle again and the butt again punishes his jaw, and he falls into the drop-off of rocks, brush, and timber.

I barely catch my balance as the warrior falls away some 30 feet downward. Instantly, I sense movement and a shiny glint to my left, as the third warrior comes flying toward me with a knife in his hand. I step back half a step, spreading my feet and bending at the knees, and instinctively, my left arm raises swinging the barrel of the rifle towards my new challenger. I hear metal on metal as the knife strikes the moving rifle, and feel a sharp pain as the knife finds a finger on my right hand. Then, the barrel finds its mark hitting the warrior's ear and head with a crack of an ax into wood. This warrior, too, slips off the ledge falling into the brush and rocks below.

Without even looking, I scramble back up the stone trough I slid down moments before. My feet slip on the loose rock, my knees and shins become banged and bloody, as I pull hand over hand up and out, to the meadow above. I run and run, my chest heaving, craving for air in my lungs. I cut into a tree line, and angle off a new direction, afraid to look back, fearful that the determined warriors are right behind.

I change directions again, running into a dry wash, a low area to stay off the high ridges, running, and running. Suddenly, my pant-leg catches on a broken limb, sending me flying headfirst tumbling into soil and prairie grass. I must have been knocked unconscious; I don't know for how long. The next thing I feel is a kick on the boot. My eyes open and two dark shadows loom over me. I shudder fearing it is the Kiowa again, but when he speaks I recognize that it's the wagon master.

"Get up kid, ya still got your hair. Found your brother and the deer. He gave up his life and his scalp for you. But you're still alive. Now do him proud. Get off your ass and get back on your job. This wagon train's going to Santa Fe."

##

Redemption

Can a young gun find redemption from the accidental injury to a child?

"Ok Clay, here ya go. Four rocks, forty yards,....now!"

BAM,...BAM,...BAM,...BAM

"Dangit, I missed the last one," said Clay as he spun the Army Model 1860 Colt into his holster. "But I done better 'n' you, Kenny."

"I'd a had four if'n I hadn't slipped in the grass here," replied Kenny."I done four last time."

Shooting river rock pebbles placed on a fallen tree down by the creek south of Sedalia, Missouri was one way to pass the time in the summer of 1865. When you're 17 years old, you try hard to prove you're a man, and one way is honing your skills with a Colt.

The civil war was over, and those boys who went off to war came back men. You could recognize them around town now. It was more than just the remnants of the blue uniform. It was their bearing, their calm confident demeanor, their scars, and bandages. They were heroes.

Clay Cannon and Kenny Mason were too young to go off to war, not that they didn't try. But the local recruiter knew the boys and knew their parents. Both of the dads, Cannon and Mason went off to fight in the great war. Mason was a casualty in the first charge at Shiloh, and Cannon died at Gettysburg, defending against Pickett's charge. Clay and Kenny were rejected by the

Redemption

Army; their duty was to family, and care of the family farms. Then, when the war was over, a captain came by the house and told Clay's ma how his pa had died a hero. He left the pistol, a cap, and a bloody shirt. Now, after finishing daily chores, Clay used that pistol every day.

Clay had tended to the farm, but his heart wasn't in it. If he wasn't down by the creek shooting, he and Kenny would go over to the Sedalia rail yards where the cattle were sorted and loaded for shipment to the east. Sometimes, Clay and Kenny would pick up some work moving the herds from the lots to the rail cars. A good night resulted in coins in their pockets, some whiskey to warm their belly, and listening to the stories of the cowboys.

"Didja hear that, Clay? They get $7 a head," said Kenny. "Man, we work a month and don't even see that."

"Yeh, that's a lot," said Clay. "Ooh, I don't feel good, that batch of whiskey tonite musta been sour, uh, uh, eayaa,..." as he turned and upchucked whiskey all over his boots.

"Get over it man. Hey! I got it. I got it." Kenny's shaking Clay on the shoulder to wake him from the drunken stupor. "That pen in the back, there's some twenty head there, didn't get loaded. Let's break 'em out of there, and drive 'em to the next station, and sell them to the yardmaster there. They'll never be missed here. C'mon, Clay, c'mon."

They led the herd out the gate and down a back path, east towards a watering station called Smithton. They had barely gone a mile when Kenny heard yells and a shot from the pursuing stockyard cowboys.

"He-yaa, he-yaa," Kenny yelled as he fired a shot back at their pursuers. The cattle began to stampede. Clay kicked his mount in the ribs to keep up with the now charging cattle. Suddenly, a carriage loomed, sitting in a crossing roadway, right in the path of the charging herd. Clay could only pull back on his reins and guide his horse to the roadside as the herd charged directly into the carriage.

In an instant, the cattle charged into the carriage, up-ending the wagon and its occupants, a man, and a young boy. Painful screams were heard through the stomping of hooves. Clay looked on momentarily, considering what aid he might offer when a shot from the pursuing cowboys splintered a nearby branch and splattered his face with wood chips. Clay kicked his horse again and escaped through the woods, leaving a tangle of human and animal bodies, and carriage parts.

Clay circled back in a westerly direction, not stopping in Sedalia. There was no way that the man and boy could have survived. Clay knew that he could not face the fear and the shame of causing the deaths of two innocent people. The boy's look of fear and the screams of pain were etched in his memory as he continued riding through the night. Though tired, he pushed on to the next day, until he found a clearing next to a creek bed just east of Kansas City. He hobbled the horse and lay on the ground under an oak tree, instantly falling asleep.

"Oh, oh, Papa, save me!" Clay woke with a start, sitting up and looking around. There were no cries now, but the image of the boy terrorized by a trampling herd of cattle remained in his head. Looking around, Clay saw orange clouds overhead and a red sun peering through the trees, and long shadows telling him that nightfall approached. Then his stomach growled and he realized that he hadn't eaten in two days. He mounted up and rode into Kansas City.

He found a saloon in the stockyard district. Cattlemen and cowboys were ending their workday with a few drinks, making deals for the next day, or sharing stories of the cattle drives and work on the lots. He ordered a whiskey, smelled meat cooking in the back, asked for a steak, and found a small table along the wall. As he ate, he overheard some of the conversations.

"Hey Clem, I'm here to collect on that drink you owe me."

"Yeh,…yeh. Hey Sammy. Need a whiskey for my man Nate, here. …Yeh, that rot-gut stuff, since I'm buying."

"Say, Clem, you hear ole man Jackson died? Rustlers stampeded a herd right into his carriage. Too bad, he was an all right boss man."

"What?... When? Where?

Redemption

"Over Sedalia way. Coupla days ago. Damn near killed his kid, too. Little Johnny. Hear he's tore up real bad. Don't know if'n he'll make it."

"Rustlers, you say? They catch 'em?

"I hear tell one was shot dead on the spot. Local Sedalia kid name of Mason. Other one got away."

Clay suddenly felt sick. He set down the knife and pushed the whiskey back to the other side of the small table, and hung his head in disbelief. The cattleman Jackson dead, Kenny dead, and little Johnny like to die. The boy's fearful face flashed once again in his memory. Clay stood, turned his back to the men at the bar, and walked slowly with rounded shoulders and lowered head out the door of the saloon.

Clay drifted aimlessly for several days through eastern Kansas, from one town to another. Several days later, he walked into the Thirst Quencher Saloon in Emporia. It was a Saturday evening, and from the laughter and sounds of the voices, it was clear that these men had a head start on the weekend. Clay stepped up to the bar, reached into his pocket, pulled out his last two bits, and ordered a whiskey.

In the midst of the laughter and boisterous talk, words suddenly became angry as two men jostled.

"Harmon, I told you to get out of town by sundown." The Emporia sheriff had stepped through the door, his hand close to holstered Colt.

"I'm collecting a debt. This here horse thief owes me," answered Harmon, his hands at the ready.

"Who you callin' a thief? Them's fightin' words," said the accused thief.

In an instant, the thief's hand jerked towards his pistol. Harmon was quicker, and with his left hand slapped the gun away from the accused thief, causing him to lean between Harmon and the sheriff standing near the door. Two shots rang out. The thief arched his back and groaned, and in an instant, the sheriff was seen kneeling at the doorway holding his stomach, blood seeping between his fingers.

Everyone froze. Harmon had used the thief as a shield to stop the sheriff's bullet, while he shot the sheriff. With his gun still drawn, Harmon started to step around the body of the thief, now laying at his feet.

"You all just stay put an' I'll be making my way out that door," said Harmon.

No one moved. Then, a voice came from the end of the bar. "Hold it, mister, you're not shooting a sheriff and walking out that door." Clay took a sideways step into the middle of the room blocking Harmon's exit.

Harmon turned his pistol towards Clay. "What's this kid doing in here? Come in for yer sasparilla, kid?" A nervous cough was heard in the back of the room. Men behind Clay and Harmon shuffled quickly away from the line of fire.

Clay held his ground. "You're not walking outta here after shooting the sheriff."

"If I was fishin,' sonny, and pulled you up on my hook, I'd throw you back in to grow a little," said Harmon with a cocky smile. His gun moved slightly with his swagger. There was a chuckle at the back of the bar, drawing Harmon's attention.

BAM.

A dull, look of surprise came to Harmon, as he looked back to see Clay's gun smoking in his hand. Harmon's mouth dropped open, and pink bubbles formed at his lips. His gun fell to the floor, and then Harmon knelt slowly and fell face-first to the floor.

"Mighty fine shootin', young man,… Ya got grit,… an' some common sense," said the sheriff, now slouched in a chair, pressing a bandana tightly into his wound to stem the bleeding. " I could use a deputy around here, especially while I'm on the mend. You interested?"

Clay holstered his gun, and remembered a few moments ago, how he had paid his last two bits for a whiskey. "I reckon I am, Mr. Sheriff, sir. I done spent my last two bits when I rode into town."

Redemption

"Yer hired. An' don't call me sir. Name's Andy. Now, one of you men fetch the doc and get me over to the office, I need to swear in this deputy.

Sheriff Andy was laid up, under the doctor's care with strict orders to take it easy until his wound healed. Clay was sworn in that day, pinned a deputy badge on his shirt, and assumed the duties that very day. Clay's courage and fast shooting, ridding the town of a trouble-maker, earned immediate respect locally. Clay had found a new home.

With civil war now over, and Kansas being a new state, the prairie towns like Emporia sitting along the westward trails began to grow. Westward travelers were passing through, cattle drives were sometimes routed through, and some folks would homestead in the area rather than pursue dreams further westward.

Clay learned quickly that work as a sheriff was not easy. While many folks would respect the authority of the badge, there was an occasional young tough who thought he was faster or bigger or just drunk enough that he was looking for a fight. Clay found that, with some skill, and common sense, he could talk down most troublemakers and send them on their way to sleep off their drunk or convince them it was wiser to leave town. Several had challenged Clay and found the hard way that Clay's fast accurate shooting left them with a busted gun and missing finger, or a broken right arm.

One day as Clay walked the streets on his daily rounds, the stage rolled into town. Clay watched as a beautiful woman stepped from the stage, and then turned to assist a young boy, hobbling with wooden crutches. The woman was strikingly beautiful, in a Kelly green taffeta ankle-length dress, fashionably spread by four petty-coats, along with matching elbow-length gloves and topped with a broad-brimmed hat. The boy, Clay suddenly realized, was the child injured by the stampeding cattle in Sedalia! What could they be doing in Emporia, Clay wondered.

Over the next several days, Clay caught glimpses of the beautiful woman with her crippled child around town. The beautiful lady was that talk of the town, particularly among the men who hung out at the Thirst Quencher Saloon. Clay learned from others that the widow Jackson and her son had moved to Emporia to manage ranch property that had been part of her dead husband's estate. Each week, they arrived in town, in an open wagon, conducting business at the general store. Their paths had not crossed, and, while not avoiding them, Clay made no effort to encounter the woman and boy.

One morning, Clay was in the stable, preparing his mount for a ride out to a nearby creek to check on a report of cattle rustlers in the area. The quiet of the morning was broken with the scream of a woman, sounds of a scuffle, a gunshot, a call for help, and then the pounding of horse hooves, heading out of town. Clay ran to the street and saw three riders racing out of town, each carrying some kind of bundle in one arm.

"Help! Sheriff! There's been a robbery!" James, the store clerk stumbled into the street, holding a bloodied arm. "They robbed the safe, and took the widow Jackson and her boy!"

The boy's crutch lay on the ground, near the wagon, and the widow Jackson's hat was in the street. Clay ran back to the stable for his horse, yelling over his shoulder to the clerk, "I'm going after 'em. Tell sheriff Andy."

Clay could see three specks and a small cloud of dust rising from the Kansas plains, about a quarter-mile ahead. By now, he knew the trails surrounding Emporia and much of eastern Kansas. He spurred his horse off the trail and over a ridge and then down into a dry wash that led towards a creek, a creek that would cross the trail about a mile ahead. He slowed his horse to a walk, as he approached a stand of willows and brush that surrounded the creek near the crossing.

The horse's ears twitched, and then Clay heard a horse whinny just ahead. He dismounted and circled the reins around the branch of a small tree. The willows and brush provided some cover, and Clay stepped forward slowly peering through the brush. There were voices, and between the trees, he could see the woman and boy standing near a tree as two of the robbers watered their horses. Where's the third one, Clay thought. Then he heard the click of a cocking pistol.

"Come join the party,…deputy. Well, well. You're the one what kilt my brother Harmon. Got me a score to settle with you." The voice came from

Redemption

behind a bush, but Clay couldn't see the man. "Step into the clearing and drop your gun."

Clay stepped around the bush that had hidden him from the two robbers watering their horses in the stream. Each quickly pointed a weapon at Clay. The woman and the boy were behind Clay, out of harm's way. Clay's mind instinctively assessed his situation, two guns faced him head-on and one still hidden in the bushes to his right, all ready to fire. But, thought Clay, only the man in the bushes cocked his weapon.

"Howdy boys, Ma'am, …son, saw the creek there, wondered if I might water my horse," he said pointing towards the water with his left hand. Heads turned towards the creek, Clay instantly spun right, drew, and fired into the bushes…BAM. He continued his right-ward turn, dropping to his knees and firing at the other two. BAM BAM,…BAM.

Clay was knocked backward, and his head and back hitting the hard ground. There was a scream from the woman and the boy, and then the sound of a dropped rifle, a dull thump, and the whinny of a horse. Then all was quiet.

Clay felt some cold water splash in his face. He twisted his head and then felt a burning pain in his shoulder. He opened his eyes and saw Sheriff Andy kneeling next to him with a canteen of water.

"Andy,…I tried to save 'em, the,…the widow and the boy," said Clay, the words coming haltingly with pain.

"Ya done good, deputy. Stood up to three of 'em," said Sheriff Andy.

"The lady, 'n' the boy,… tell 'em I'm sorry. Real sorry. It,…it was me and the Mason kid what kilt Mr. Jackson." Clay coughed up blood and felt really tired. "I,…I done my best to save 'em."

"I checked you out kid, knew it was you. But your work as a deputy, and this here, ya got all three, ya done redeemed yourself."

"I,…I got all three?" Clay died with a smile on his face.

##

Spanish Eyes

Will a traveler find love in a cantina, or must he fight for his life?

"Ten,…fifteen,… twenty. Good job, men."

Cody Collins flexed his sore muscles, quickly recounted his pay, and folded it tightly into a pouch under his belt. Cody, and the other two teamsters, had just completed a three-wagon delivery of supplies and merchandise from New Orleans to Austin. A month's pay, for three weeks of work. Not bad for a lean, muscular nineteen-year-old.

"Monday morning, crack of dawn for the return trip. Right here," said the freight master over his shoulder as he settled accounts with the merchant.

"Yes sir," said Jake, a seasoned teamster who'd worked this route before. Turning to his young co-worker, he asked, "Hey Cody, what say we head out to that place I was telling you about, Conchita's Cantina?"

"Sure thing," said Cody as he patted his hidden money pouch. His mouth watered in anticipation. "Where is this place?"

"Bout ten miles west of town, out along Barton Creek, over on the Mexican side." Jake pumped up his chest and touched the Colt at his side. "Sweet senoritas out there."

Texas had declared its independence from Mexico in 1836, and then in 1845, it had become the 28th state of the union. During this time, most local Mexican natives remained in the area co-existing with the Americans, each in

Spanish Eyes

their own sections. Now, in the late 1860s, as reconstruction moved the country past the divisiveness of the civil war, the Mexican – American relationships ran warm and cold. Whiskey, of course, often sparked the intensity of this cultural intercourse.

It was near mid-night when Cody and Jake tied their horses outside the cantina. Inside there were voices and laughter, including some female giggles and squeals. They stepped into a dimly lit room where vaqueros stood in small groups at the bar or seated at several tables. Two lanterns behind the bar provided enough light to reveal that Cody and Jake were the only two Americans in the room. At a corner table, two dark-haired Mexican girls giggled and tittered on the laps of two vaqueros. A thin veil of smoke hung in the room, from the cigarros of the vaqueros.

"Bienvenidos amigos," said the bartender. Then switching to English, "what would you like to drink?"

"Whiskey, my friend, two of your best," Jake responded.

The girls giggled at a remark by a vaquero at their table, and Jake turned his head to look. Cody watched with interest, but suddenly felt the silent glare from the bartender. Then, there was some commotion from the end of the bar as a man stepped out from a back room. His hand held what looked like a small squeeze box accordion device. He gave three quick stomps of the foot and began moving his arms to pump the accordion, producing a quick-paced stuttering beat of music.

"Aie-yaaa, musica, el conjunto," said the bartender as he rose a glass of whiskey in the air to salute the musician.

The girls swayed to the music, each pulling their partner to dance the open area in the center of the cantina. While one man danced with his girl, the other vaquero held on to his glass of whisky and his cigarro, pushing the girl away.

She stamped her feet and pouted briefly, then twirled and danced over towards Cody and Jake. She was a black-haired beauty, with a smooth olive complexion, exciting dark eyes, and inviting lips. She danced and swayed to the oompah beat of the music; her colorful muslin dress did little to hide her soft petite body revealing curves and womanly virtues that fired Cody's imagination.

I'm in love, thought Cody. The girl spun past Cody and glided away, leaving a momentary aroma of sweetness in the air. She moved like a woman, yet seemed child-like and innocent. The motions of her dance seemed to Cody to be gestures inviting him to join her on the dance floor. Their eyes would meet, and she would step close, only to tauntingly spin away out of reach. The strong whiskey warmed his stomach.

The next thing Cody realized, he was spinning and dancing with the beautiful black-haired girl. When the music ended, he felt dizzy, the room seemed to be spinning around him and he stumbled. The girl caught him holding him steady. They held each other close. Cody inhaled her perfume and looked into her beguiling eyes.

"I'm Cody," he said breathlessly. "What is your name?"

"Hola Cody," she smiled as she touched his strong shoulders. Her eyes fluttered. "Me llamo Carmelita."

Suddenly, Cody felt a tight grip on his arm that jerked him around, and a fist slammed into his jaw. He stumbled backward, and then he felt hands drag him out the door and fling him to the ground.

As he flew through the door, he heard Carmelita scream, "Diego, basta, basta ya!"

Cody awoke with a pounding headache, a tongue that felt like boot leather, and a sore jaw. His clothes were damp from the dew on the grass where he lay. Water splashed over rocks nearby, he heard a high-pitched twitter overhead. Looking up he glanced at the yellow-headed songbird he recognized as a golden-cheeked warbler that flitted through the trees.

"Oh, my head. Wha,...what happened?"

"Damn, man. I thought you were dead. You gave'm a good fight though," Jake said, nodding his head approvingly. "You remember any of it?"

"I was dancing with an angel,...and then,...I was grabbed or bumped or something. And now here I am feeling like the dregs of a stampede." Cody stood slowly, weaving, arms spread for balance. He made his way towards a copse of willows near the creek, stepped behind a tree, and took a leak.

"Those vaqueros took our horses. Boss is gonna be pissed, gonna take it out of our pay. I gotta get back to Austin for the return trip." Jake was shaking his head as he thought about their predicament. He lit a cigarette. "You coming, Cody?"

"Uh, no, not yet. I'm going back,...I gotta see little Carmelita." Cody's eyes dreamily drifted skyward.

"Those boys didn't like you dancing with that girl. Just find them horses and hi-tail it," said Jake as he started walking downstream back in the direction of Austin.

It was near dinner time when Cody walked up to Conchita's Cantina. He peeked through a small side window but did not see Carmelita inside. Disappointed, but hungry, Cody stepped into the cantina and saw several vaqueros at the tables eating dinner.

"What do you want?" The bartender's voice was cold, there was no smile in his greeting this time.

"Umm, wondering if I might get some dinner, uh, like they're having over there," Cody said, pointing to the Vaqueros. "What are they having?"

"Enchiladas y frijoles." The cold stare remained.

The memory of the lovely Carmelita flashed back to Cody's mind. Determined, he held his ground and met the stare head-on. "Yes, enchiladas and frijoles. And a whiskey. I'll sit over there."

A few moments later an elderly Mexican woman brought food to Cody's table, set it down, and retreated silently back to the kitchen. Then the bartender stepped up to Cody's table, hand extended, gesturing for payment. When Cody had paid, the man placed a glass of whisky on the table. Cody finished his dinner and had another whiskey.

As the evening progressed, a few more vaqueros came in, and then several young women arrived about the time that a guitarist and the conjunto player began to play some music. As long as the music continued, the women continued to dance, finding a partner for a few dances and then another. Even Cody was enticed to a few dances by one young lady named Rosita. She seemed nice enough, but Cody kept looking around the room hoping to seek the dark-eyed Carmelita.

"I know you have eyes for Carmelita," Rosita breathed into Cody's ear as she snuggled close during a slow dance. "But Carmelita is betrothed to Diego. Diego, he brings gifts to Carmelita's father."

"But she asked me to dance,…I can tell she really likes me," Cody replied as his eyes quickly scanned the room again.

"Diego,…he is fast with the gun, you risk death to dance with Carmelita." Rosita squeezed his hand and pulled him close. "I make you happy."

After a while, the musicians took a break; when the music resumed, the dancing began again. It was then that Cody saw Carmelita and another girl enter the cantina, their hips already swaying to the music. She stopped briefly to talk with a vaquero. Anxious to put his arms around this exciting girl, Cody stepped forward, taking Carmelita by the hand.

"Hi Carmelita, can we dance? I've been waiting for you." He led her to the center of the dance floor.

"Hola Cody. ¿Como está? Hi Cody, how are you?" Carmelita's eyes sparkled, her smile beamed.

Cody answered by pulling Carmelita close, inhaling her sweet aura as their feet moved with the fast-paced music. There was a commotion at the doorway, but Cody was oblivious, lost in the sensuousness of his dancing partner. As Carmelita began a spin in their dance, a hard hand grabbed Cody's right arm and flung him into a table, which collapsed under his weight, spilling Cody to the floor.

Spanish Eyes

Men gasped and women screamed. The music stopped. Everyone stared at Cody as he stumbled, trying to get quickly to his feet. Diego stood over him, hands at the ready, a low slung pistol on his hip.

"Outside, gringo! You touch my Carmelita, you die!"

"No, Diego, no, por favor," Carmelita pleaded tearfully, reaching to hold back Diego's right arm.

Diego pushed Carmelita back and he stepped forward over Cody. Cody's foot slipped as he tried to get up while backing away, falling over a chair. Diego reached in and grabbed Cody by the arm and pushed him out the door.

Flung through the doorway, Cody stumbled into two horses tied at a hitch near the entry, falling into a muddy puddle of horse urine. Cody came up swinging, landing a right to Diego's jaw and then a left to his midsection. The vaqueros had spilled out of the cantina, now cheering their member in this brawl over the attention of the lovely Carmelita. Cody's six-foot frame towered over the shorter Diego, whose stocky bull-like stature seemed immune and unscathed by the punches. Cody's wave of furor stretched through his long arms and extended reach, continually swinging at the shorter man, who ducked and parried the blows. With each swing and parry, Carmelita and the other girls would gasp and shriek.

The exchange of blows continued for fifteen minutes, or more, to the delight of cantina patrons, reacting to each connected punch. Now tiring, the fighters stumbled towards a nearby copse of trees. Finally, Cody connected on a blow to Diego's midsection followed by an uppercut to the jaw, knocking the vaquero over a deadfall tree stump where he remained.

Bloodied and sore, Cody walked back towards the cantina. Then he saw tied behind the cantina, the two horses he and Jake had ridden the day before. He went to retrieve the horses, leading them to the front of the cantina, where he saw Carmelita, in tears, comforted by her girl friends. Cody approached.

"Carmelita, I,…I want you to come with me, away from here."

"What? What do you mean?" Carmelita's eyes showed concern, questioning.

"I, …uh,…I love you, Carmelita, I want to marry you, I want you to come away with me."

Carmelita's eyes moved past Cody, and her mouth dropped silently. Her eyes grew in fear and her hand rose protectively to her throat.

"Gringo! Now you die!"

Cody turned suddenly, seeing Diego, standing some ten yards away, legs slightly spread, hand poised above the low slung pistol on his hip.

"Draw, gringo!"

Carmelita gasped, her hands coming to her lips. Cody's heart ached, he wanted so badly for this girl to be with him. A love so great, he had to fight this man to take her away with him. Cody's hand flinched, pulling at his Colt…

BAM…BAM

It felt like a horse kick in the chest, and there was a puff of dust in front of his feet. His pistol fell to the ground, and there was the metallic taste of blood in his mouth. His knees gave way. Lightheaded, now he was kneeling in the street, watching red drops puff in the dust. The next thing he knew, he was laying on the ground, his head cradled softly, and his eyes fluttered open briefly. Feeling his strength fading, he looked up into Carmelita's dark sad eyes, welling up with tears.

"Te amo, Cody."

##

The Spirit of Sonora

Is it experience or a higher power that guides a young Texas Ranger?

The wind kicked up a swirling dust-devil, causing the rangers to hang onto their hats, and hold the reins tightly to keep the horses from pulling away from the stinging sand of the Texas plains. Captain Michael McLeod led the group of four Texas Rangers, trailing a band of horse thieves who had two days head-start out of San Antonio.

The wild mustangs had been rounded up from the west Texas highlands by an enterprising rancher and penned on the outskirts of San Antonio for selling to the local settlers in the surrounding area. In a daring daylight raid, local outcast Bobby Randolph and his band of troublemakers had sprung the gate, and while one jumped his horse into the makeshift pen to spook the mustangs and then guide the herd of some 25 wild horses back to the western Texas hills. A couple of shots were fired, but all that remained was a cloud of dust by the time the rancher arrived on the scene. Randolph's band even cut loose the ranchers' ponies, thus preventing pursuit.

According to witnesses, there was a new member of Randolph's band, a Comanche half-breed known as Flying Hawk. Flying Hawk was credited with jumping his mustang pony over the rail and spooking the heard to run to the open gate.

The dust devil passed and McLeod, a fifteen-year veteran ranger, now five years a Captain, pressed on. The mid-morning sun promised another 100-degree day in the Texas hill country. While this was considered to be one of the most beautiful regions in the area, with its rolling hills, spring-fed rivers, and lakes, the sub-tropical climate of central Texas in the summer brought long periods of drought drying up the seasonal vegetation.

"Looks like they're headed into the high plains out past Sonora way," said McLeod. "Leading 25 horses, it's an easy trail to follow and they're not making any effort to cover their tracks." Close at his side, young 19-year-old Travis Taylor, recently joining the force as a new ranger, shadowed the Captain and listened to his mentor. In addition to demonstrating skills in horsemanship and handling a firearm, Texas Rangers were expected to be experts at tracking with the persistence to get their man, traveling light, living off the land, and being ever alert for the dangers on the frontier.

Travis had noted that McLeod carried a gold piece in his pocket, and often fingered it, rubbing the coin between his thumb and forefinger, before heading into danger or a tense situation. McLeod was doing that again as the group neared Sonora. "They're nearby," said McLeod, "I can feel it. See here…" he said pointing to the tracks in the hard sandy soil, " the pace of the herd has slowed, they're walking now, and two riders have split off this way following that wash down to a dry river bed."

McLeod directed the two experienced rangers to trail the herd." Keep your Colts at the ready," he cautioned. The rangers each carried two of the "Walker Colts," a specially designed five-shot revolver with a percussion firing system. The Walker Colts had been designed by Ranger Captain Sam Walker and built for the Ranger service by Colt, one of the leading arms makers of the day.

The revolving cylinder design had been instrumental in saving a ranger team in a recent battle with the Comanches. The rangers beat off an attack by warriors because of the repeat firing capability of the revolver handgun. The Comanches, accustomed to a longer re-load process from flintlock weapons, had attacked after the rangers fired their first volley, only to be cut down by the five-shot revolvers.

"I sense they're nearby," whispered McLeod over his shoulder to Travis, the team's newest young ranger. He slowed his horse to a walk, and his right hand casually slipped loose the rawhide loop that held the Colt in its holster.

Travis copied the actions and slowed his horse to drop back about 20 feet behind the Captain. They rounded a bend in the dry river bed approaching a ridge covered in mesquite juniper brush and a scattering of large stones. Their eyes panned the ridge, gully, and rocks out to the horizon. Then Travis's horse nickered and the animal's ears twitched slightly.

Suddenly, ahead, McLeod was rolling from the saddle just as a shot rang out kicking up dust in front of Travis. Travis's horse reared from the shot, and Travis instinctively used the horse's upward lurch to launch himself from the saddle and jump into a nearby gully. Gun in hand, Travis tried first to locate McLeod, and then to find the location of the shooters. A shot came from the riverbed ahead, spitting dust as it ricocheted off a rock on the mesquite ridge. Travis heard a scramble of footsteps ahead, then a second shot again splitting branches in the mesquite and a yelp of pain. There was a rustling in the mesquite and then two more quick shots, and a screamed curse. Then silence.

Unable to see McLeod or the shooters, Travis stayed crouched in the gully, his pistol at the ready. Then there was a whistle, and Travis saw McLeod's horse appear and begin the climb to the mesquite ridge. "Travis…Git up here" called McLeod. Travis cautiously worked his way up the ridge, squeezing through the sharp branches of the mesquite. Near the top of the ridge, he came to a clearing and saw two dead rustlers. "This one's Bobby Randolph, tried to bushwack us," said McLeod as he casually re-loaded the Colt.

They rode on, following the westerly slope of the dry bed. Travis noticed McLeod once again fingering the gold coin. Reluctant to ask about the coin directly, Travis queried, "Captain, I saw you dodge that shot, how'd you know they were there and when they'd fire?"

"Fifteen years of trackin' Comanches and white scum," replied McLeod, adding, "experience, thinkin' like 'em, listening to my horse, and a little help from the Spirit. Saw a metal glint up on the ridge, and the Bay twitched his ears in the same direction…thought I'd better take cover. Heard your horse nicker too, …you catch that?" Travis shook his head, realizing he still had a lot to learn if he was going to keep from being killed, a necessity if he would continue as a ranger.

Riding on in silence, Travis considered McLeod's remarks. *A little help from the Spirit... what did he mean by that?* Travis nudged his horse alongside McLeod. The mentor, aware of Travis' approach, maintained his horse at a steady purposeful walk, while he continued to survey the ridges, valleys, and horizon for signs of the bandits. Travis's thoughts materialized, haltingly at first, "Captain, ... er... what did you mean a little help from the spirit?"

McLeod glanced sideways at the young Ranger, and then his eyes checked their rear and then circled the horizon as if checking to see if others were in hearing range. McLeod spoke softly, almost a whisper, "been in this area before, years ago, as a young Ranger, much like yourself, but on a mission alone. This is the area of the Sonora Caverns. These horse thieves likely plan to hide out in the caves."

Travis leaned in to better hear McLeod's words over the clumping of the horse's hooves on the hard soil. Again scanning the horizon, front and rear, McLeod continued, "back in forty-two, tracking a renegade from Mexico, he'd killed a homesteader an' run off with his stock and came through the Sonora area like the bunch were tracking now. The trail led into a deeply eroded wash, and then just disappeared. Circling to find the trail, I stumbled into a hidden entrance to these caves,...they call 'em the Sonora Caverns. Came across an ancient trapper, a spry old guy."

McLeod again checked their rear, and scanned the horizon, as he reached into his pocket and pulled out the gold coin. "He gave me this...said it served him well for eighty-one years, helped him to recognize the friendlies, and to avoid the hostiles. He called it 'the Spirit of Sonora,' says it will look out for you, he'p you through tight spots. He said it was time to pass it along." Travis watched McLeod again fingered the coin as he had before.

" It's saved me more than once," observed McLeod. "It gives you a sixth sense, you read sign, you seem to sense trouble before it happens. Sometimes that extra second or two makes a difference." The riders had stopped as they examined the shiny yellow coin.

A deep croaking sound belched from a nearby mesquite bush behind them, and both riders instantly spun in their saddles and palming their Colts. A black

The Spirit of Sonora

raven hopped down from a branch in the mesquite and grabbed a tiny lizard attempting to flee into its hole. Another belched croak was heard overhead as a second raven glided to the ground for a share of the tasty morsel. *It's a sign*, thinks McLeod, and he says, "kid, I'm back here again, by these Sonora Caverns. I've come to be open to these signs and to respect the Spirit of Sonora. Here, kid,..." McLeod flicks his thumb under the coin, spinning it in the air to Travis. "It's time to pass this along to you."

Late in the afternoon, McLeod and Travis picked up the trail of the stolen herd, and then came upon the other two Rangers. The group stopped near a creek bed to rest the animals and eat a light meal of dried beef and stale flatbread. Due to the proximity of the rustlers, the meal was washed down with water rather than start a cooking fire for coffee which might give away their position. As the group ate, McLeod circled the area staying behind the ridges to check the location of the rustlers and to plan their approach.

"Get some rest now, guys," McLeod said upon his return. "We'll break camp an hour before dawn, and hit them before they awake," he instructed as he sketched the bandits' camp and surrounding lay of the land with a stick in the dirt. The Rangers slept on the ground, wrapped into their bedrolls for warmth in the cool arid night.

A thousand stars twinkled in the dark moonless night. Travis had a fitful sleep, recalling the surprise attack from earlier in the day, and the foreboding anticipation of similar gunplay in the coming morning. He fingered the golden coin, stowed it in his pocket before finally drifting off to sleep. During the night, a vivid dream foretold of a surprise attack and death. Travis kept his Colt handy, holstered under his bedroll, instinctively drawing the weapon when a horse nickered and a coyote howled during the night.

A hint of gray showed in the east, as McLeod kicked the feet of each man and gave a low whistle. "Let's move...quietly," McLeod breathed in a loud whisper, directing the two Rangers to ride south towards the herd, and motioning to Travis to follow him on foot towards the rustler's camp near the entrance to the Caverns. The area was rugged with low ridges and deep gullies washed by the run-off rivers that raged following seasonal storms. Ahead, Travis caught a whiff of a faded campfire, reduced to glowing embers from the day before. McLeod signaled Travis to the left, while he circled to the right.

Crouched, and stepping lightly, Travis cautiously moved towards the camp area in the darkness, pistol in hand. The sky showed a light gray on the eastern horizon, just enough to make out rocks, bushes, and obstacles. Off to his right, Travis heard a rustling sound. He froze in his position, cocked Colt at the ready, finger alongside the trigger guard. There was a muffled cry, again to his right, then silence. He slowly moved forward, inching toward the still sleeping bandits.

"Look around – behind you," Travis spun and sensing movement coming down upon him, and thinking, it's McLeod, warning me. Travis instinctively squeezed the trigger, and the barrel flashed. He was knocked to the ground and a sharp pain cut his left arm. He heard an exhaled grunt from the dark figure that suddenly disappeared into the bushes. His shot had awakened the camp; the drowsy rustlers were grabbing their guns and looking around. Travis quickly focused and placed two quick shots which found their marks downing two rustlers. Galloping horses approached, and suddenly the remaining two rustlers had dropped their guns and held their hands high as the mounted Rangers entered the camp.

Travis turned around, looking for McLeod, thinking the Captain must have been just behind him to call out a warning of the leaping attacker. McLeod was not around, but Travis did note some blood on the ground, suggesting that his shot had found its mark. Travis cut arm was evidence that his attacker had used a knife, but broke away when shot. As Travis reunited with the Rangers, they discovered McLeod stabbed and mortally wounded, his last words saying to be alert for the half-breed Flying Hawk.

The Rangers wrapped up the job by burying their Captain and marking the gravesite because he had no known family. Then they tied the rustlers to their saddles and rounded up the mustangs to be herded back to San Antonio. The trip back had been un-eventful, the rustlers had accepted their fate and, once a lead stallion mustang was identified, and tethered to one of the Ranger horses, the herd took the direction to follow his lead.

To Travis, however, the quiet return trip seemed too good to be true. He was unsettled that the half-breed had escaped, and likely was still out there, waiting for an opportunity to strike. About a day's ride west of San Antonio,

The Spirit of Sonora

they made camp near a stand of willows alongside a stream. A couple of ropes looped around several trees created a small corral for the mustangs who stayed near the leader stallion. The rangers agreed that Flying Hawk's escape prompted the need for a sentry and each took a turn.

Travis took the final guard shift, about two in the morning. He quietly circled the camp, and then crouched behind a stone that gave a view of the camp and the horses. A first-quarter moon gave enough light that, after his eyes had adjusted away from the fire, he could see shadows, shapes, and movement. Travis sat still and listened, and found his fingers stroking the coin in his pocket. A distant coyote howled and another replied, but the horses remained settled. Later, Travis heard a screech owl, back in the trees, then a few minutes later, a closer screech.

An image of McLeod flashed in his mind, and McLeod's last words, *be alert for the half breed.* The hair on his neck stood up, and Travis slowly drew his Colt and quietly clicked back the hammer. His eyes scanned the camp and the horse corral. A horse nickered, and then the stallion stomped and several other horses stirred. McLeod's voice again materialized, *"Look around – behind you."* Travis spun around the boulder, sensing...feeling a dark flash and catching the shiny glint of a knife. Rolling back with the gun above him, Travis fired at the moving shadow. The half-breed's buckskins glowed in the muzzle flash, and Travis again heard the muffled grunt as the attacker fell by the rock. Determined, Flying Hawk's knife came up again slitting Travis' pant leg. Travis fired again and the attacker fell motionless.

Upon returning the stolen horses to the San Antonio rancher and bringing the remaining bandits back to stand trial, Travis reflected on the mission. He recalled the surprise flying attack used by Flying Hawk, the half breed; his name was very fitting. Saddened at the loss of Captain McLeod, Travis fingered the coin in his pocket and considered the providence of the whispered warning that had twice saved his life. It must truly be the Spirit of Sonora.

##

Soldier's Heart

Can a Captain overcome war stress to lead his troops in battle?

"Cap'n,…Cap'n,… where'd they go?"

"Shut up, an' keep watchin'," barked Captain Titus Barnes as he crouched behind a dead horse, looking around nervously over the grassy plain below. "They're out there, in the grass, waiting, watching."

"Don't see 'em," said 19-year-old recruit, Private Archer as he rose to a standing position to look down off the small ridge where the soldiers had taken refuge in a hollowed dip, a now dry buffalo watering hole that collected water in the rainy season. Hoofprints made by buffalo in the rainy season now made bumpy ridges in the hard soil that caused the soldiers to squirm uncomfortably as they tried to hide behind a slim three inches of soil and grass.

Whiff. Whiff. Two arrows flew by. "Huuh," gasped Archer, as one arrow sunk into his stomach, its barbed arrowhead protruding from his back. The young soldier looked numbly at the arrow and his now bleeding midsection. Blood trickled from his lips, his face turned whitish gray, and he collapsed into the circle of six fellow soldiers who huddled behind tufts of grass in the small hollow,

"Stay down, you idiots! Stay down!" BAM, click, click, BAM. Captain Barnes fired his lever-action Henry repeater down the hill aimlessly at the waving blades of prairie grass. "Dammit!" Barnes cursed as he saw young Archer writhe in pain. Another young recruit, Tibbets, began sobbing as he lay

Soldier's Heart

next to his dying friend. Tibbets' shoulder was bloody, having been nicked by an earlier arrow when the troop had been ambushed by the band of warriors.

It was spring of 1867, a few short months after Oglala Lakota chief Red Cloud had massacred a cavalry troop from Fort Phil Kearny under Captain William Fetterman, an uprising that was now referred to as Red Cloud's war. As the young soldier gurgled his last painful breath, Captain Barnes cursed his own stupidity, for pursuing a small band of warriors who had attacked the supply wagon train being escorted by troops under his command, only to be drawn into an ambush. Though remaining hidden in the surrounding prairie grass, the attackers now yelled taunts to the entrapped soldiers.

Barnes's mind flashed back, some two and a half years before, to a crowded entrenchment on the southern fringe of Franklin, Tennessee. Confederate General Hood had engaged the dug in federals in a fierce onslaught. Then a Lieutenant, Barnes directed a company of soldiers manning a forward outpost, in front of the main lines defending the city. Barnes' 80 soldiers had fought valiantly, against persistent day-long infantry assaults, and exploding artillery fire. Memories of the deafening noise, smothering smoke, and anguished cries of wounded and dying soldiers flooded into Barnes's consciousness as he closed his eyes and hung his head into the dusty prairie soil.

"Cap'n,…Cap'n, they're coming." Tibbet's high pitched voice projected his paralyzing fear.

A fierce looking warrior popped up seemingly from nowhere, and came screaming, charging towards the small huddled circle of blue-clad soldiers. Wearing only leather leggings, a breechclout, and moccasins, the warrior's face was painted in reds, yellows with black marks. The muscles of his chest and arms flexed as he raised a spear, running and screeching towards the cowering shocked soldiers. In a flash, he leaped into the huddled circle, smacking the wide-eyed frozen Tibbets on the face with the spear, making a large gash across his cheek, then stabbing the broad-brimmed cavalry hat from the head of Archer, and in a continuous motion sprinted with his prize over the dead horse and back into the cover of the tall grass.

BAM, click, click, BAM. Captain Barnes had now risen from his momentary stupor and fired his Henry repeater in the direction of the now disappeared warrior.

"Wha,…why didn't he kill me," mumbled Tibbets.

"Counting coup," answered the Captain, as his head turned around to survey the location of the attackers.

"What?"

"Counting coup. It's a demonstration of a warrior's bravery, that he can come into our midst, touch us, and escape unharmed," explained the Captain. "And now he has a prize, Archer's hat. The others will now demonstrate their bravery as well. Their prize will be your scalp."

"Keep shooting," growled Corporal Davis, a soldier who had experienced battle against the Confederacy, and now on the plains. "Find a target, make 'em pay."

Whiff, thump. An arrow flew into the huddle and stuck into the shank of the dead horse. Captain Barnes flinched and gasped uncontrollably. Then scattered gunfire erupted from the invisible attackers on three sides.

"Aaahh! I'm hit." Captain Barnes rolled into a ball and clutched his thigh, now bleeding from a bullet wound. "Oww! Oww!" Barnes's body twitched uncontrollably. His mind flashed again to the devastated entrenchment near Franklin when a cannon fired a round of canister instantaneously killed three Union troops and put multiple shrapnel wounds into Barnes' body. Now, Barnes gasped for breath, wheezing as he instinctively tried to get air into his lungs.

Next, a flaming arrow dropped into the dry grass and the flames took hold, fed by the winds, and began to blow smoke and fire towards the huddled soldiers. The thick smoke began to choke the soldiers, now trapped by fire on one side and a stream of bullets and arrows from the other side. The Captain's wheezing, now led to a coughing fit because of the thick smoke.

"Captain Barnes! Captain,…take hold," called the Corporal. The Captain continued to shake, in his tightly curled position. "Captain,…take hold," repeated the Corporal. This time he jammed the butt of his Spencer carbine into the Captain's fanny. The jolt seemed to startle the Captain back to the present reality.

"Franklin, ... Rebs killed my squad,...happening again."

"Here, take my kerchief,...bandage your leg," said the Corporal to his superior. Taking charge, Corporal Davis turned to the others and barked an order. "Check your ammo, reload,...watch your field of fire, make each shot count."

Following the direction, the soldiers intensified their fire, holding the warriors at bay. The flames were drawing nearer to their small circle, and the smoke was thickening. Suddenly, there was a gust of wind downhill, pushing the smoke and flames in the direction of the attackers.

"Captain, winds turning in our favor, I see a horse yonder uphill. I propose we make a break for it, Sir," Corporal Davis suggested. "Perhaps, Sir, if I used your Henry, I'll cover our escape."

Captain Barnes grimaced in pain, glanced at his huddled troopers, and the blowing smoke and fire. He gritted his teeth, nodded, and then handed his 15-shot lever-action repeating rifle to the Corporal. "Load your weapons, boys, Corporal's gonna cover our escape."

The soldiers reloaded, and at the Captain's "GO," they scrambled from the low trough up the rolling hill towards the loose cavalry horse standing in the distance. The Captain hobbled, favoring his injured leg, using the Spencer as a walking stick. Davis cut loose a barrage of fire with the Henry as his fellow soldiers ran through the smoke.

By evening, the soldiers had returned to the supply train. Corporal Davis stopped by the wagon where Captain Barnes was now resting his re-bandaged leg.

"I'll take the eleven to two watch, sir. How's your leg?"

"Flesh wound, Corporal. I'll live." The Captain hesitated momentarily, then spoke in a hushed tone. "About today,..." the Captain gestured with his hand as if to push away a flying insect, "you performed well today, Corporal.

Demonstrated leadership under fire, we won't speak of it further. When we get to the fort, I'm recommending you for promotion to sergeant."

"Yes sir, thank you, sir." Davis looked down towards his feet and spoke softly, "Soldier's Heart, sir, I been there too."

##

Dying Wish

Will the townspeople honor the final request of their well-regarded sheriff?

"Do you think he'll make it? He was shot up real bad."

"Got 'im settled in my backroom behind the store. Shot twice,… in the thigh and in the chest, purty close to the heart," said Clem, the general store proprietor. "Doc's makin' 'im comfortable. Don't give 'im much hope though. "

Kevin O'Leary wiped the bar with his bar towel and shook his head as if he were trying to erase the memory. "Them Corrigan brothers were a bad bunch. It started right here in the saloon." A muscular man with bull-like shoulders and tree trunk arms, Kevin walked with a limp, due to an injured leg acquired in charge at Shiloh, and earning him an early discharge. Lumbering out to the center of the saloon, he righted two chairs that lay scattered on the floor from the barroom tussle moments before.

Kevin continued, "The mean one, Colin, refused to pay Gerti, here, after she brought drinks to their table. I came around the bar, but Sheriff Robertson must have been passing outside because he came in and dragged Colin out by his ear to the street. Course, the others followed."

"Scared the livin' daylights out of me," Gerti shuddered, still trembling in her fear. Now pale as a ghost, her rouge was streaked from tears and her blue taffeta dress now torn exposing a white petticoat below, bore evidence of the altercation.

"Then, I heard the ruckus and looked out the door of the store," added Clem, trying to add his bit to the story. "Sheriff Robertson stood up to the three of them, out there on the street, told them to get out of town. Well, Colin, he's near 250 pounds, he gets up like he's going to swing at the Sheriff, and then he just freezes, you know, a stalemate. Well, the others, they froze too."

Kevin picked up the story. "And then that hotheaded one, Darrell, he goes for his gun, and then there's a fast flurry of shots and there's the four of them, lying there bleeding in the street. Just smoke, 'n dust, 'n four bodies right there."

Four red circles could be clearly seen out the window. Drag marks showed which way the bodies were removed. The undertaker's wagon moved slowly down the street.

"Oh my, Oh my," Gerti gasped, still unable to control her emotions as her friends relived the shootout. Her eyes glistened and tears dribbled down her cheeks again.

"Gerti, love, get that bottle and pour another round, on the house. It's been a tough day. Then I need you to wash those glasses in the sink," said Kevin, trying to keep his saloon girl busy so that her emotions would keep in check.

In the late 1860s after the end of the civil war, communities were trying to get back to the way it was before the war. And the people in the community of Uvalde, Texas, like those in other southern towns, yearned to return to the old days. Trouble was, the south had lost the war and the union had imposed its rule, by sending northerners in to manage law and order. Carpetbaggers and profiteers had followed, disrupting the order of things in southern life. But, the western areas like Uvalde didn't experience as much of the reconstruction interference as the communities in the old deep south.

The regional military commander had appointed former Union army sergeant Chris Robertson to be sheriff of Uvalde. Robertson didn't talk much about his military experience, but it was known that he had a commendable record with the cavalry under General Sherman at Chattanooga and then promotion to sergeant and a leadership role in the march through Georgia to Atlanta and on to the sea.

Dying Wish

A person of small stature, Sheriff Robertson quickly gained acceptance through a firm but even-handed control of the disruptive elements that plagued western towns in the 1860s. Most problems centered on disputes and fights that seemed to begin after a hard day of drinking in the local saloon, and the tracking down of horse or cattle thieves. Robertson's cavalry experience was apparent to all in this little town. Though handy with a navy Colt and the breech-loading Spencer carbine, Robertson was more than likely to resolve problems with wits and common sense.

Clem's wife, Martha, a portly woman, had now arrived. Sniffing her nose and dabbing damp eyes with a hanky, Martha was trying hard to maintain control as she sat at the table with the men. The small group in the saloon began to regale each other with their memories of Sheriff Robertson.

"Ya know," said Kevin, "Chris wasn't a big man, but he sure made his presence known and got the troublemakers to settle down. I never saw a lawman so quick with that navy Colt but didn't seem to have to use the gun. He'd say a couple of words, ya know, …sharp insightful words, …to put those boys in their place. Brings to mind how mother O'Leary used to keep her 8 children in line, even when we was growed up."

"When you're fast with the gun, it does the talking for you, I guess," added Clem, as he slugged down the last of his whiskey. "He was a crack shot with that Spencer, even while riding. I guess it was that cavalry experience showing through."

"For a man out here in the west," added Martha, "Sheriff Robertson was mighty kind to the tribulations of us ladies. More than just tippin' his hat and saying howdy ma'am. One time I was upset about a,…a lady issue, I won't bore you gentlemen with inappropriate details, but Sheriff Robertson seemed to have observed the situation and understood my problem, and offered a practical suggestion."

Gerti had returned from behind the bar, calmer now, poured another round of drinks, and then joined into the discussion. "I agree with you, Martha. Sherriff Chris was a special man,…Oh dear! Listen to me. Speaking like he's already gone. I mean to say he is special. He understood the issues I deal with, you know, frisky men sparking at me. He offered some sure-fire ways on how to put a misbehaving man in his place."

The group laughed with Gerti, all recognizing that, as a saloon girl, she was often the object of overzealous affection by drunken cowboys. Gerti's husband had died the Siege at Vicksburg, and she now struggled as a single woman to make a living on her own.

"But, that Sheriff Robertson was a man I could cotton to," added Gerti, fingering the whiskey bottle as she talked. Her finger dabbed a drop of whiskey from the lip of the bottle and she put it to her lip, and then her tongue swished across her lips. An attractive woman of 38, the language of her body spoke silently and with greater clarity than the words from her lips. The others watched, in anticipation, knowing that Gerti had more to say.

"I mean, he was a protector and all. And not afraid of those big men, even when they're drunk. They scare me sometimes. But Sheriff Robertson, he just stood up to them, and put them in their place." Gerti paused again, and her finger seemed to find another errant drop of whiskey which was dabbed to her lips.

The others patiently smiled, as Gerti continued. "Ya know, I asked Sheriff Robertson to come back to my place one night,…" Gerti blushed bright red as this secret was revealed. Clem glanced at Kevin and winked, as these two men silently observed Gerti's surprising disclosure.

Gerti's hand quickly covered her lips as if to try to pull the words back into her mouth. "But he was a gentleman and he turned me down," she said and then quickly turned and ran to the backroom in embarrassment.

Embarrassed as well, Martha sought an exit from the discussion. "I'm going over to the store to see if there's anything I can do to help Doc."

Moments later, Martha returned to the saloon, her face ashen, tears on her cheeks. "Chris is dead. But there was one final request. I,…I don't know how to say this. Chris had a final wish, asked to be buried in the,…the red gingham dress hanging in the window of the store,…"

"What! What did you say?" asked Clem in amazement.

Dying Wish

"It's true. Can't deny a person their last request," said Doc as he appeared at the door of the saloon, his sleeves rolled up to his elbows, with his hands and apron stained red with blood. "You see, Chris was short for Christine, not Christopher. I knew Chris during the war. Family lived in Gettysburg. Lee came through. Some Confederate soldiers, drunk, killed Christine's husband and child. After they was buried, Christine put on Yankee blue, fighting as a man, hunting Confederates until she found the ones that killed her husband and child."

"I'll be durned," said Kevin as he dried a shot glass and placed it on the shelf.

"Funny thing," added Doc. "Today, Chris settled that score. Corrigans were the ones what killed her family."

"Good to know I ain't lost it,…never been turned down by a man before," deadpanned Gerti.

##

Caleb's Courage

Can a young soldier overcome his fears in the face of the enemy?

Caleb stirs, a searing pain bears across his forehead from ear to ear. His back and arms throb like the time he was thrown from a spooked horse, and the pressure on his chest makes each breath a difficult task. A warm liquid seeps into his eyes, yet unopened, and he senses the musky dryness of dusty soil, and a pungent strange new smell registers in his mind. In the distance, a rumble brings to mind a passing thunderstorm. Nearer, a crow caws.

It must be time to wake up, Caleb thinks, perhaps I overslept. Eyes flicker open and catch a flash of brilliant blue sky but squint quickly blinded by the mid-day sun. A heavy weight bears down on his mid-section, as more senses return, the salty smell of sweat, a taste of blood, and the feel of a woolen jacket. Rising to his elbows, and pushing at the heavy jeans cloth jacket, Caleb again opens his eyes. There is a scream, Caleb jumps up, pushing at the jacket, suddenly realizing the scream was his own and the jeans cloth jacket contains the mangled body of a fellow Confederate soldier.

Now standing, his heart was pounding, with a raspy breath frantically keeping pace. Backing away quickly, trying to distance himself from the dead soldier, Caleb stumbles and falls over what seems to be a soft log. Landing hard on his rear, Caleb realizes that he has fallen over yet another dead soldier. Standing again, now afraid to breathe, his eyes circle the field, taking in twenty, no… thirty, no … forty or more dead or dying soldiers. Every one stained in red, lying in strange positions. There are Union soldiers and

Confederate, some appearing to be staring blankly skyward, others missing a hand, or a leg, with dark pools of murky brown spots surrounding the wounds. In the distance, someone moaned and he could hear another dying soldier crying for his mother.

Standing there breathless, suddenly salivating, Caleb feels a surge of bile and a heaving from his stomach, then bending forward and retching what must have been his last meal.

Realization breaks though. Caleb's friends and neighbors, young men like himself, formed just two months ago into the 2nd Texas Infantry Regiment, committed to a 180-day enlistment and anxious to defend against those Yankees who wanted to break the economic back of the south. How exciting it had been when the enlistment officer came to south Texas, speaking of the duty and glory to fight to protect the state's rights and the Confederacy. He told of the great victories at Fort Sumpter and Bull Run, and said that volunteers were needed to replenish the ranks.

Reluctant at first, Caleb had followed older brother Joshua, and neighbor Jimmy to the recruiting tent in Houston. The Army had set up a large training camp, with tents, supplies, and groups of men mustering into the army, receiving butternut tan uniforms, caps, belts, and a haversack to carry supplies. The units were organized from the Houston and Galveston areas. Caleb observed that the young men assigned to his battalion were boys from surrounding counties, some of whom he had attended a nearby school during the winters and who had worked on the ranches and farms in the area. Joshua had helped teach Caleb to ride the old mare, and the brothers had pitched in when neighboring farmers helped Jimmy's family raise a barn in 1858.

Due to the shortage of rifles, most of the new soldiers brought muskets from home. Those without a weapon trained in marching, and field maneuvers using sticks or carved wooden toy rifles. But Caleb, Joshua, Jimmy, and the others, raised in the 1850s on the prairies of central and southern Texas were no strangers to the muzzle loading muskets and rifles of the day. By age 10 or 12, every boy had accompanied his father or an uncle onto the prairies or into the wooded glens to shoot squirrel, Canadian geese, or hopefully a deer for a bountiful meal, or had chased away the troublesome coyotes.

Captain John Creed Moore was designated as the leader of the 2nd Texas Infantry. A West Point graduate, Caleb learned that Captain Moore had resigned from the federal army and joined the confederacy to defend the south. Captain Moore told the Texas boys that they would be getting British-made Enfield muskets upon assignment to a unit near the battle zone in the east. The idea of getting a new musket was part of the excitement of going to war.

But now, after awakening among the dead on the field of battle, that excitement was gone. Caleb looked around again, seeing the lifeless bodies of his friends, fellow soldiers who now lay dead in the fields at Shiloh. Unable to hold back, Caleb again felt another heaving surge of bile; he gagged and coughed producing only spittle and soreness in his throat. A crow cawed once again and landed near the body of a fallen fellow soldier. The crow began to pick at the soldier's open wound, at a bloody shoulder where the arm had been blown off.

"Get out of here…get away from him," yells Caleb, grabbing and throwing a stone at the crow. The crow hopped back to dodge the stone that bounced in the dust. Mocking Caleb, the crow let forth a raucous caw and hopped back up on the solder's body. Caleb waved his arms, yelled, and stepped towards the body; in response, the crow flapped its wings and lazily flew up and across the field of death alighting now near a body in the blue jacket of a fallen Yankee soldier.

Caleb went in search of his unit, following a trail of debris, blood, overturned wagons, damaged caissons, bodies of soldiers, and an occasional dead horse. The trail of death led to the north, towards the Pittsburg Landing. In the distance, he could still hear an occasional rumble and boom of cannon. Then distant rumbles stopped; the silence and stench of death became overwhelming.

Walking on looking for his unit, Caleb's memory of the day's events begins to return. The regiment had approached Shiloh through a grassy field from the south after a 4 days march in heavy rains to Corinth to join the General Jones Withers' army in Mississippi. They had arrived exhausted, wet, and sore. They were issued supplies of powder, horn, wadding, balls, and two days supply of hardtack, but the promised Enfield's had not yet arrived. They were instructed to make camp at the southern edge of the field, about 100 yards from the wood.

Word was that the Yanks were in the area near Pittsfield Landing, but confidence was high and the experienced soldiers said in a day or two they would be chased from the area. It was April 6, and Captain Moore had ordered troops up to be ready for battle. Near the wood line, there some popping noises, a yell of surprise, and then more popping and a cry of pain.

"Sound call to arms. Grab your weapons!" screamed the Captain. "Form up, form up," the voice was hoarse, with an edge of excitement. Sleeping men scrambled from their tents, dropped skillets and forks, stumbled over tent pegs, grabbed their muskets and powder and ball. They were ordered to charge, and quickly the Texans were closing fast on the Yankee line, Minie balls flying past their ears like angry bees. Then, from the charging hoard arose a blood-curdling scream, all of them, making the neck hairs stand strait. Caleb recalled the talk of the guys who had already been in war, this was the rebel yell, intended to scare the hell outta the enemy.

But, the yanks stood fast and fired back. Suddenly, a fellow soldier fell, first one, then two, some silent, some screaming. Caleb heard a dull thwack and saw friend Jimmy spin around. But there was no left hand, only a bloody sleeve, his eyes and mouth wide open, blood at the corner of his lips, but no sound come out. Another thwack and Caleb was splattered with blood. Caleb's legs refused to move, his arms frozen. A warm liquid ran down his leg and wet his trousers. Caleb's mind flashed to younger fun-filled days with Jimmy, and then a deafening explosion threw dirt in their faces and slammed Jimmy's bloodied body against Caleb. Together, they fell to the ground and all went dark.

Now, walking, stumbling along under the heat of the mid-day sun, Caleb's throat is parched, his lips and tongue like saddle leather. He finds what looks to be the road to Pittsburg Landing and pushes his legs forward step by painful step, following a trail of litter and blood. Ahead there are soldiers, milling about a dilapidated old barn. As he approaches, they look up, their ashen faces and hollowed eyes showing the image of devastation. This war, once eagerly anticipated by green untested boys playing soldier, now settles into a new reality of dismemberment, destruction, and death. A few yards past the barn,

Caleb sees some familiar faces, some of the guys from the 2nd Texas. Up against a tree, sitting on the ground, there is brother Joshua, dirtied, with a bloodied rag tied around his right arm. He has a captured Springfield across his lap. In recognition, they both smile, relieved to see that each is OK.

Caleb hesitates as he approaches, recalling the overwhelming fear that caused him to freeze in the face of the enemy, a fear so profound that bodily functions fail and the only response is to urinate. The image, now clear in his mind, as Yankee soldiers took defensive positions, aimed their Springfield's and fired at the advancing Texans, his legs were frozen in an imaginary mire while hands seemed disconnected causing the musket to be a useless 8-pound weight. Caleb looks down at his blood-stained boots, convinced that the others must have seen his fear, a fear so shameful that he could never face family and friends back in Houston; a fear so shameful that he believed he deserved to die.

Caleb recalled that standing right next to him, boyhood friend Jimmy valiantly aimed and fired his rifle at the enemy. But for his valor, a Yankee bullet found its mark ripping away Jimmy's hand splattering Caleb's face with his blood, and a cannon shell exploded nearby slamming both to the ground. Jimmy's body accepted war's punishment, and now Caleb must live with the memory of his fear and failure as a soldier. As he approached Joshua and the guys from the 2nd Texas, even though they don't speak it, Caleb can see in their faces the knowledge of his failure.

It is now April 7th; a new day dawns, with the memories of yesterday's battle still stinging. The quiet rustle of a stirring camp is disturbed by a bugle's "call to arms." Captain Moore, with greater confidence in his voice, calls "form up! Form up! Assume firing positions." The yanks begin a counter-attack. Caleb now has a captured Springfield, one that looks dinged with battle scrapes, scars, and the blood of the previous owner. He loads and cocks the rifle. This time we're ready. Coming over the hill we first see a red and white guidon, then bayonets extended from the tips rifles, then heads a hundred across, then the blue jackets of Yankee soldiers.

"Hold fire! Hold fire! Wait for the order," calls Captain Moore. The blue line breaks to a run, and they too begin to scream. Caleb feels his heart pounding, his rifle is up, aiming at the line, finger quivering near the trigger. They're nearly upon us… it's impossible to breathe…their screams are deafening…

"Fire! Fire! Fire at will," screams the Captain. Caleb's rifle sites on a boy carrying the guidon, suddenly there is a flash in his face, and the rifle jerks. In the blue line ahead, a boy stumbles, the flag slips from his fingers to the ground, a red blotch appears on his chest and he falls. Smoke fills the air and the odor of gun powder burns the nose.

Caleb screams, "I did it! I did it! Got to reload…powder in the muzzle… minie ball and wadding … ram it in… powder in the pan…cock the hammer…here comes another screaming yank…Fire!"

##

The Last Score

How high are the stakes for simple train robbery?

"When we gonna get there, Ma?"

The small girl fidgeted in her seat looking out the window, and then she turned around to face her mother and father. Just then, the train car jerked and rocked, jostling the family from side to side. Puffs of gray smoke and an occasional spark blew by as the smell of the burning wood permeated the rail car. The rhythmic churning of the locomotive's large wheels could be heard and felt as the train pulled its load up the long incline into the Wyoming mountains.

"Soon, sweetie, soon," said her mother, pulling a small bundle of string from her handbag. "Here, sweetie, why don't you play cat's cradle?"

"Like to arrive in Salt Lake late this evening, maybe dinner time," said the girl's father, speaking to his wife, rather than to his daughter. The mother and daughter wore matching floor-length blue taffeta dresses with white ribbons tied in a bow in their hair. The father, a well-dressed merchant, sporting a string tie with his starched white shirt and pinstriped suit, complimented his family's stylish appearance that spoke of their aristocratic roots in Chicago.

Across the aisle, Garrett Tolliver smiled as he watched the family's discussion. Even though the Union Pacific trains now connected Chicago to San Francisco, reducing travel across the great prairie and mountain ranges from two months down to eight days, children were still impatient travelers. The train jerked back and forth again, shaking Garrett back to the reality of this trip. A detective with the famed Pinkerton Agency, he had been hired to investigate a recent string of train robberies affecting the Union Pacific line. He hoped that the safety of this young girl and her family would not be threatened by violence on this trip.

Garrett had alerted the train's engineer and conductor of his presence when he boarded in Omaha. After conferring with the mail agent, and inspecting the express car with its $40,000 mine payroll secured in a safe, he determined that he would ride unannounced as a passenger traveling to San Francisco on business. He carried a Chicago newspaper as a prop for the portrayed business purpose of his trip.

An attractive young lady, two seats up, had been observing the little girl's conversation. She had smiled at Garrett before turning her attention to the scattered trees and rolling foothills as the train rocked and rolled through the beautiful wilderness. Garrett nodded an acknowledgment to the lady's smile, recalling that she had introduced herself as "Miss Jefferson, a teacher," traveling to Salt Lake to take a new job. His calm friendly demeanor and businessman's appearance belied a man ready for action. Hidden under his wool coat, he carried a six-shot Colt 38 caliber pocket pistol, in a custom-made shoulder holster, with a derringer holstered in his right boot, and a Bowie style knife in his left boot, both covered by loose-fitting trouser legs. A Henry lever action 15 shot repeater was stowed with his bag in a luggage compartment of the rail car.

The little girl, guided by her mother, beamed proudly, having manipulated the string on her fingers to create the desired crisscross pattern. Garrett rose casually and strolled to the front of the car and then back through the second passenger car to the express car. To fellow train riders, he appeared to be taking a stroll to stretch his legs. In reality, he was checking all the passengers looking for signs to identify an accomplice who was sometimes placed on a train to create a distraction at the time and place that the robbery was planned.

Upon reaching the express car, Garrett knocked at the door using the prearranged signal. Over the clacking of the train's wheels, he heard the timber bar slide away and saw the upper half door open. The express agent who rode within the locked car peered out.

"Howdy, Jake."

"Afternoon, Mr. Tolliver. See anything suspicious?"

"Nope. Checked passengers. Several boarded back at Laramie, but no obvious confederate. If trouble's coming, it'll likely be on this last leg, before we come out of the mountains and into the valley by Salt Lake,"

Four men sat on horses looking down the ridge towards the curved track below. A quail whistled its distinct "bobwhite" call in the distance, saddle leather squeaked and a horse stomped its foot sensing the anticipation of its rider. One man coughed and then spat phlegm to the ground. Their leader, Jedidiah, gruff-looking and trail dusty with two days of beard growth surrounding a ragged handle-bar mustache, glanced at the sun's high position and then down at the rounded shadows under their horses, taking one last drag on his rolled cigarette. He squeezed the stub of his smoke in his gloved right hand, while his left hand held the reins between his thumb and palm, having lost the fingers of his left-hand years ago fighting a Sioux warrior with a tomahawk.

"Let's git down there. Train's due by within the hour. Got ourselves a mine payroll to pick-up," said Jedidiah, glancing again at the sun. "You got the powder, Pate?"

"Yep, powder, fuse, lights." Pate coughed and spit once again, as the horses trailed in line down the steep hill behind Jedidiah.

In the distance, a smoke trail from the train was now visible, heading towards the narrow draw below. Upon reaching the track area, the men set up near an old tree that stood near the tracks.

"Pack half of the powder there, at the base, away from the track," Jedidiah growled pointing with his stubby left hand towards a gnarled old tree, an ancient Douglas Fir. The old tree leaned precariously towards the track, scarred by a burnt gash of a recent lightning strike. It needed just a slight nudge to tip the old tree across the tracks to block the passage of the train. "Run the fuse to that gully, and wait there for my signal. You other two hide in the trees over there."

The Last Score

The bellow of smoke and blow of the steam engine could be heard from behind the steep hill as the train approached the narrow draw where the robbers had set up their operation. The ground trembled, the horses shook their heads and snorted nervously as the rumbling iron monster neared. Smoke was seen through the tops of the trees, and then the train rounded the curve approaching the old tipping fir. Jedidiah waved his kerchief and Pate lit the fuse.

The train rumbled on belching its steam and smoke, closer towards the ancient fir. Horses stomped and trembled, their riders tightly pulling back on the reins to control the scared animals. Closer,…closer,…

BOOM!

Dirt and bits of grass and bark and wood chips showered the area and rained upon the waiting robbers. Slowly, the old fir tipped over to a horizontal position leaning from the hillside over the tracks like a gate. A smokey gray and dusty tan cloud rose from the base of the tree. A small flame was seen in the dry brush on the uphill side of the gaping hole where the finger-like roots now reached skyward.

Wheels screeched as the engineer tried to bring the train to a stop. It was clear that the impact with the tree would damage the train's boiler and chimney. The engineer was able to bring the train to a stop within 10 feet of the ancient tree now blocking its path.

Inside the train, women shrieked in fear, and the little girl fell into the aisle and began crying. Garrett recognized immediately that the explosion created blockage or track damage requiring an emergency stop by the engineer. Before the train had fully stopped, he was on his feet, holding on to the seatbacks as he worked his way to the door. As he reached the doorway, he was met by the barrel of a Winchester 73. With the gun barrel in his face, Garrett stepped back into the passenger car holding his hands at his waist, palms open and forward, suggesting to the intruder that he was not armed.

"This is a hold up" the robber growled. Then he gestured to Garrett, "you, Mr. Do Gooder, don't pay no mind to what's goin' on outside. You take this hat and you hep me relieve these folks of money, jewelry, and guns."

Garrett eyed the man coldly, then held the front of his wool coat open slightly to show that there was no gun belt at his waist while keeping the pistol in its shoulder holster still hidden under his coat. He accepted the hat and turned slowly down the aisle gesturing to individuals to place valuables into the hat. He could hear the robber's feet shuffle behind him and feel the barrel of the Winchester, as it moved from side to side as an encouragement to the riders to give up their belongings.

"Its,…its all I have, my life savings,…" cried Miss Jefferson, the teacher, tears streaming down her cheeks, when Garret stood before her holding the hat.

"Put it in there lady, or this rifle comes along that pretty face of yourn," threatened the robber.

Garrett nodded to the teacher to encourage her compliance. The little girl was crying as her mother and father dropped belongings into the hat. As they reached the back of the car, Garrett could see into the car behind that another robber was doing the same thing there as well. Outside, Garrett heard a shot and then a voice calling that the engineer had been hit. The women in the car began crying again. Garrett turned and faced the robber holding the hat so that the valuables could be seen between them. The man's eyes went down to the valuables, and he reached with his right hand to grasp a gold pocket watch that lay on top of the items.

Just then, Garrett dropped the hat between them, his right hand grabbed the Winchester, and a left-handed uppercut slammed into the robber's jaw. The robber grunted and blood appeared at his lips as Garrett pulled the rifle from the man's grip, slammed the handle into his groin, and then used a left cross to down the man, leaving him unconscious at his feet. Garrett pulled the derringer from his boot and handed it to the Chicago merchant.

"Here, it's cocked, ready to fire. Watch him, shoot if he tries anything." Garrett stated with authority. The merchant nodded. Garrett turned to the other passengers, " You others, stay inside here."

Just then, there was another explosion and the train shook. Women shrieked and men gasped. It was back by the express car, Garrett thought, they are trying to get to the safe. He used the commotion to exit on the opposite side and run along the track-bed to the back of the train.

At the back of the train, Garrett checked the Winchester for its load, and then patted the Colt under his coat for reassurance. He lowered to his knees and slowly peered around the freight car at the end of the train, checking for where the robbers would be. A smoke cloud hung near the express car. One robber was attempting to tie a rope to the damaged but still closed sliding door while another sat on a horse with the rope wrapped around the saddle horn, apparently planning to pull the damaged door from its track. The engineer sat grimacing in pain on the ground near the tender, shot in the leg, while the fireman nervously attempted to comfort his friend.

There was something strange, about the robber on the horse. Garrett observed that this robber tended to favor his left arm or hand as if it were injured, relying entirely on his right hand. As a man whose life often depended on a quick assessment of individuals and the danger they presented, such observations were instinctive, lifesaving. The individual attempting to tie the rope to the door struggled, following orders from the man on horseback. And, Garrett recalled, he had seen that there was another robber in the second passenger car.

The rope was now secure, and the horseman kicked his animal to pull. The rope became taught, there was a creaking sound as the wood and metal slides strained and weakened. In a moment, the blast weakened door would give under the pressure, Garrett had to act now.

Garrett aimed the Winchester and squeezed the trigger. BAM!

The Winchester exploded in his face and split as the barrel and the stock flew in two directions, leaving Garrett temporarily blinded, deaf, with his left hand feeling numb. The robbers froze, staring in surprise at the explosion by the rear of the train. The taught rope snapped, as the door gave way, causing the robbers to turn in the direction of the express car. The horse stumbled as the rope pulled the door to the ground.

Garrett recovered, drew his Colt, and fired at the horseman. He saw flashes of a quick series of shots and felt a sting on his left arm. The horseman fell, and Garrett turned his aim at the gunman who had emerged from the second passenger car. Their eyes met and guns simultaneously spit flames. Garrett felt like he was kicked in the shoulder, spinning him around and onto the ground.

"Garrett,…Garrett, you still with us?" Jake, the express agent knelt over Garrett with a look of concern.

"Wha,…What happened?" Garrett looked up at the blue sky and fluffy clouds, his hearing had returned.

"Why,…Garrett, ya done saved the day," said Jake. "Ya kilt one, other one's shot-up pretty bad, like to cry for his mother. The one you knocked out is tied up, and I got the one at the door. Your shooting saved the train and saved the payroll. We got to tend to that shoulder."

"The one on the horse, …did he make it? I've got to talk to him." Garrett grimaced in pain as he pulled himself up to a sitting position. "Help me up."

Holding on to Jake's shoulder, Garrett stepped slowly over to where the robber with the stub hand lay moaning. Garrett looked down at the man, noting his left hand missing its fingers. His memory flashed back to an Indian skirmish on the plains years ago. He squinted his eyes, trying to focus on a fuzzy image, now beginning to feel faint from his shoulder wound.

"Jed,…Jed,…is that you?"

"Gare? Is that you Garrett?" The wounded robber blinked his eyes open. "Holy mother of God!"

"Jedidiah! Little brother, what are you doing here? Seems I'm always cleaning up your messes."

"Gare,…Gare,…promise me, will ya, It was gonna be one last score. Then I was gonna go straight…." The front of his shirt now soaked in blood, the wounded robber, Jedidiah Tolliver coughed and spit up blood. Garrett was now kneeling next to his mortally wounded brother, who he hadn't seen in three years.

The Last Score

"Gare, promise,…promise me ya tell Ma that I went straight,…" He coughed once again and his eyes rolled back under his eyelids.

"I,…I promise, little brother," Garrett whispered, his eyes moistening.

##

Fool's Gold

Released from prison, can a man re-start his life?

"Here come de gimp,…here come de gimp."

The keyring rattled, the lock clicked its release and the jail door squeaked open. The guard walked with a limp, injured from an inmate melee years ago. The words of one now became a chorus.

"HERE COME DE GIMP,…HERE COME DE GIMP."

"QUIET!" yelled the guard, as he banged a chain against jail bars. "Jerrod Conners, git up! You're outta here. Now!"

The inmates at the prison in Fort Leavenworth, Kansas, quieted quickly. Jerrod Conners rolled over in his bunk and winced as pain stabbed in the old wound in his shoulder. He looked up in disbelief. There were six more years on his sentence for killing an express agent during a train robbery in 1870. The men cheered as Jerrod was manacled and led from his prison cell out the locked doors towards the warden's office.

"Mr. Conners, it is not my decision; I believe your deeds deserve full term. However the governor has seen fit to issue an order of clemency," said Warden Tibbetts. A small balding man of pale complexion and dour expression, the Warden explained, " your term is reduced and the remaining 6 years are forgiven. You are hereby released. Sergeant, take this man for release processing."

Fool's Gold

Jerrod stepped through the opened gate onto the street in front of the Leavenworth prison, free for the first time in nine years. He squinted as the bright sun glared into his face, holding his hand to shade his eyes. Government-issued shoes were tight, and the shirt and pants were baggy and loose. But, on the free side of those walls, the sun showed brighter and the morning air was clearer, cooler. Jerrod wandered idly and then found himself stepping through the batwing doors of a saloon.

"Whiskey," he said as he stepped up to the bar.

Conversation stopped. Others looked on knowingly, a con, just out of the pen. The bartender poured slowly and gestured for money first before sliding the drink across the bar. The first one burned his throat, but ooh, that felt good. By the second, a plan was set. He thought, *"I'm the only one who survived the shoot-out. Piece of lead still in my shoulder, but I know where the stash was hidden."* Jerrod needed to catch a stage up to Lincoln, then, take a train on to Cheyenne.

The stage for Lincoln left at one PM. A woman with a young boy boarded at the last minute, and the boy kept staring at Jerrod.

"Johnny, stop staring. It's not polite."

"Yes'm."

"G'd afternoon ma'am, son. It's no problem ma'am," said Jerrod.

"He's a prisoner, just released, ma'am, Best leave'm be," said the other passenger, a man with a pinstriped suit, white shirt, and string tie.

Damn, thought Jerrod, as he glared hard at the man. *It's like I got brand on my forehead. I gotta get me that gold, and get some decent duds, get a little respect!*

In Lincoln, Jerrod bought his ticket for the trip to Cheyenne, but the train didn't leave till the next day. With a couple of dollars left in his pocket, he found a saloon to slake his thirst. Come midnight, as the saloon cleared out and his money was gone, he realized that he had no place to stay. A drunken cowboy stumbled past Jerrod and bumped his sore shoulder. Jerrod started to swing but held back as he saw the six-shooter dangling from the cowboy's belt.

The cowboy stumbled down one street and then cut through a back alley stopping behind the livery stable to take a leak. When the cowboy was done, Jerrod stepped from behind a nearby tree and swung a broken tree limb like it was an ax, knocking the drunk out cold.

"I'll just borrow these," said Jerrod as he unhooked the drunk's gun belt and Colt. He found a few coins in the man's pocket. " And by the way, thanks for the drinks you bought tonight."

Jerrod made his way to the edge of town and slumped down next to a spreading oak tree to rest his weary body. The next thing he knew, sparrows twittered excitedly in a nearby juniper, and the sun was rising in the east. His stomach growled and his head ached from last night's whiskey. Jerrod found an out of the way spot where he could stay hidden and watch the approach of the train; he would board the train at the last minute.

The train ride was uneventful, and Jerrod slept most of the way. One time he stirred, and he thought he saw the man in the suit walking through the train car. Upon arriving in Cheyenne, Jerrod went to the Four-Bits Saloon, hoping to find an old friend.

"I'll have a whiskey. Say, does a sweet young thing name of Katy still sing and play the pianny here?"

"Who? Katy? Don't know no Katy. Pay up, mister." The bartender wanted the money first. Jerrod was still wearing the prison-issued duds. "Try the Shave-Tail Saloon, down by the tracks.

Jerrod found the Shave-Tail and stepped in. It was dark, dirty, with a rough crowd, causing Jerrod to flashback to the prison yard at Leavenworth. In a back room, he saw a flash of red hair in the dim light and stepped quickly in that direction.

"Katy! Katy! It's me...."

"Jerrod? Oh Jerry, ah, I didn't know you were out."

Fool's Gold

"HEY RED! GIT TO WORK. YOU GOT PAYIN CUSTOMERS!" The bartender looked like an ox, a neck the size of a tree trunk, arms like rain barrels. Jerrod instinctively stepped back.

"Jerry, come by tonite. Back door. I get off at twelve."

Jerrod walked away, glancing back at Katy. She seemed older, worn, tired. Katy had been his sweetheart. He was gonna ask her to get married after the big score. He'd do it now. He'll get the gold from the stash and take her away. Maybe go to Californy or Oregon.

Jerrod waited anxiously in the back alley at midnight. Inside he heard the bawdy laughter of men and alcohol, and an occasional feminine squeal, a squeal that sounded like Katy. Finally, at about one, she came quickly out of the backdoor and down the steps, followed by a drunken miner. Jerrod stepped up and pushed the drunk who stumbled back onto the stairs. Jerrod took Katy by the hand and led her away. Later, they were cuddled in the straw in the loft of a stable.

"I don't like you working there. Bad people there, treat you awful."

"You know I love you, Jerry." She snuggled closer and kissed him softly. "But you was sent away,...a girl's gotta earn her keep."

"I'm gonna take you away from all this." Jerrod touched her chin and looked into her eyes. "I,...I got money now. Take you to Californy."

"Just leave? Just like that? You promise?" Katy's eyes moistened. A tear dripped down her cheek.

"I've got the gold from the train robbery. I know where it's hidden. Tomorrow. Tomorrow night at midnight. Meet me in the alley again."

That night, Jerrod walked the silent streets of Cheyenne, his mind racing, too excited to sleep. He needed a horse. No, he needed two horses, but the prison release money was all gone. He'd go up into the mountains, to the stash, get some gold so he could buy the needed supplies. But it would take all night if he climbed the mountain on foot. If, only...

"Go home and sleep it off!" The bartender threw a drunk cowboy onto the street in front of the Four-Bits Saloon. The cowboy struggled up to his feet

93

and stumbled to a horse standing at the tie in front of the saloon. The drunk stumbled into the horse, causing it to whinny and step back nervously.

"Here, let me help," said Jerrod as he loosened the reins from the tie while staying hidden on the other side of the horse. In an instant, Jerrod leaped up into the saddle, jerked the reins, and kicked the animal's flanks, and the horse bolted away. The drunk fell backward, laying in the street. Even though it was well past midnight, a partial moon provided some light, and Jerrod guided the horse up a familiar trail to his stash in a cave by the creek several miles up into the hills.

By morning, Jerrod was back into town. The stolen horse was tied a short ways back in the woods out of sight. He stopped first at the livery stable to buy a horse, saddle, and bridle for Katy. Then he started walking down Central Avenue towards the general store. At midday, Jerrod stepped out of the general store onto the avenue, a new man, sporting store-bought trousers, shirt, bolo tie, tailored jacket, boots, and broad brim hat. His pockets jingled with gold and coins as he strutted down the avenue towards the Four-Bits Saloon. He'd show them. Now they'd respect him. Heads turned as he walked through the batwing door; conversation stopped.

"Bottle of your finest whiskey,... Now, my man, I'm thirsty."

"Yessir. Tennessee Bourbon." The bartender put out a glass and the bottle; it was the same man who had insisted on payment first the day before.

Jerrod shifted his weight impatiently and glared. After a moment's hesitation, the bartender poured the whiskey into the glass. Then Jerrod placed a $20.00 gold piece on the bar. After several drinks, his cheeks were flushed and his courage was bolstered. Jerrod marched out of the bar, down the street to the Shave-Tail. He stepped in and looked around until he saw Katy.

Katy stood in a back corner at a small table cleaning bar glasses. Jerrod marched over, took her by the elbow, and turned towards the door. Glassware fell and broke.

"Let's go, Katy."

"Wha…Jerry?"

Fool's Gold

"Hey Red! Where ya goin'? Git back here!"

Jerrod, with Katy at his arm, strode through town. Heads turned, people on the street stopped to watch. Although attired in a tattered dress of a hireling, Katy held her head high, running on her toes to keep up with Jerrod's long strides. They reached the horse tethered at the stable, mounted together, and rode out of town towards the hills.

"The stash is right up here, Katy; in a cave around the bend. Bought you new clothes, too." They were on the two horses now. As they approached the cave, a man stepped out.

"Looking for this?" It was the man in the suit with the string tie; the man from the stage and then the train. He was standing over the wooden chest of gold, gun in hand. He quickly raised the pistol towards Jerrod's chest. "We been looking for it too. Appreciate your cooperation in leading us to it."

"You're under arrest, young man." The local sheriff stepped forward. " Apologize, ma'am. Gonna have to postpone your trip."

"But,...but, I done my time. Uh, I just found this here stash," Jerrod stammered in disbelief.

"Us Pinkertons get our man," said the man in the suit. "You left a trail of crime, assault, robbery, and horse thievery. Then flashing your riches around town today. Why, I'd call this fool's gold."

##

It Takes a Woman

Will a mountain man who is trailing kidnappers succeed in rescuing a woman?

"Too rich for me blood," said the miner, in a distinct Irish brogue, as he laid his cards face down on the table and scooped up his remaining two gold nuggets. "I'm tapped out."

"Unfortunate, my dear man. It's been a pleasure, as always." The portly man in the dirty sweat-stained white suit and red vest quickly pulled the nuggets and coins from the center of the table to the pile just inches from his round belly. "Perhaps your luck will be better tomorrow."

The dejected miner stepped back from the table, his red hair and beard, both long and matted, reflected the rough dirty life of a gold prospector seeking his fortune in the California Sierras in 1850.

"Who'll be next,…in the game of chance? Opportunities abound. Build your fortune here rather than digging in the muck and the mud." His chair moaned as the 300-pound man leaned forward to bite into a goose leg, dribbling grease onto his jowls, then splashing it down with a glass of whiskey and wiping his double chin with his sleeve. His eyes locked onto a man entering the bar. "How about you, sir? A game of chance? Leverett Laramore the Third, cousin to the Duke of Willowshire, at your service."

"That fatso never worked a day in his life," said Mike Raeburn to the local fellow standing next to him at the bar in Placer Place. Placer Place was a roadhouse saloon – general store catering to gold miners, sitting along a road

It Takes a Woman

through Auburn, midway between Sutter's fort in the California central valley and the Sierras to the east. They watched as Laramore drew another unwitting sucker into the card game. When the cards were shuffled and bets laid down, Laramore looked up around the room and gave a subtle nod. A crusty weathered old coot shuffled over to Laramore and placed a new glass of whisky on the table. Their eyes met in a conspiratorial glance, and a raised eyebrow.

"You cheatin' me?" Laramore's arm exploded across the table, with a pocket pistol appearing out of nowhere just inches from the face of the third player. The man's arms and hands quickly went up and a "no-no" was silently mouthed as his head shook left and right.

"Ain't an honest bone in his body," said the local. "He's the one cheatin', but he's accusing the other."

"Who's the confederate,…the old coot?" asked Mike. "I trailed him up from Sutter's Fort."

"Old guy's Ebenezer,… part of a pack o' thieves,…claim jumpers, I hear tell."

The next morning Mike was up at the crack of dawn, listening to the trill of a flock of chickadees high in the pines as he stoked the coals of his campfire to heat some coffee. A morning mist shrouded the treetops, as the day slowly lightened. With grayed hair, weathered skin, and a sun-creased countenance, Mike had spent most of his 60 plus years on the prairies and mountain slopes, living off the land as a trapper, hunter, trail guide, and friend of the Indians. Drawing on charm, wit, and natural instinct that comes with living in the wild, this mountain man was as comfortable facing the day after a night in a native teepee or a bedroll under the stars. Tracking an animal, or trailing a man, it was all in a day's work for Mountain Mike.

Mike reflected on the circumstances that had led him to this quest. Ebenezer and another ne'er do well, called Jackson, had tried to steal the family fortune of the prominent Trainer family of San Francisco. They had attempted to steal a gold shipment from a riverboat after its departure from

Sutter's Fort downriver to the city. Guards had thwarted the theft, but in the confusion, Ebenezer had pushed daughter Anne Trainer off the boat where partner Jackson was waiting onshore, in hopes of demanding a ransom for her return. Anne began to sink, weighed down by her long dress and petticoats. Jackson had pulled the struggling woman from the water and spirited her away. Before the guards discovered his role, Ebenezer had departed from the boat at the first ferry stop and then met up with Jackson and his hostage in a trek to the mountains. The Trainer family had retained Mountain Mike to find Anne because of his tracking and trailing skills.

James Trainer, Anne's brother insisted on coming along on the search. Mike began his tracking along the shore of the Sacramento River in the area where the abduction occurred. He had found evidence of a campground, where two horses had been tethered, and a trail that lead eastward towards the mountains. The trail had turned cold at Auburn, but the sighting of Ebenezer in the roadhouse confirmed that he was on the right track.

"Oh, sore back,...is that coffee I smell," groaned James, finally stirring as the aroma of coffee filled the air. "I miss my bed in the City. Why can't we stay at Placer Place? At least they have beds there."

"Those walls have ears, my friend," replied Mike as he poured the steaming brew into two tin cups. "There's a gambler in town, working the saloon, he's behind this, likely has spies all over,...I need you to stay in camp right here, one more day."

"Why? Anne's my sister! I should be there with you, bustin' noses, getting 'em to spill the beans."

"'Fraid not, my friend," said Mike in his slow mountain drawl. "One look at you, in those city slicker duds there, you would raise their dander,... spook 'em. I'm watching 'em like a bobcat on the prowl, in the background, outta sight. 'Nother day or two in the saloon, listening, and watching. Soon, ole Ebenezer will lead us right to the girl. Then we'll pounce when they're not expecting it."

It Takes a Woman

The next day, Mike visited the Placer Place and learned that Leverett Laramore the Third had pulled his card game and left that morning. The corpulent gambler and the skinny Ebenezer had been seen together at the livery stable. Mike struck up a conversation with the stable owner seeking details of his morning customers, but upon learning the inquiry related to the gambler, the man suddenly clammed up and walked away. Mike persisted, and a pebble-sized gold nugget refreshed the man's memory.

The stable owner revealed, "that there gambler feller, mighty big man, he needed a heavy bay draft horse. I had one with white stockings."

"And the other, the old coot?" Mike persisted.

"That old guy. He had had his own horse, a mare. He kept her here for a couple of nights. Ah, it was a chestnut mustang. Broken rear shoe. Too cheap to pay me to fix it. He'll pay in the end."

Mike checked the stables, to examine the track of each horse. The broken shoe horse was on one of those tethered down by the river where Miss Trainer had been captured. Mike now knew which tracks to follow.

He met up with James and then headed to the eastern road out of town and into the mountains. A short while later they paused where a path broke away from the main trail. Mike stepped down from his horse to check the tracks. Just to his left, his Kentucky long rifle was propped up against the tree, and the Arkansas toothpick was hung handily in a leather sheath on the right hip. He turned to his traveling companion.

"Readin' sign,... they passed by here about four hours ago. See here, heavy imprints carrying the big man, and a broken shoe on the other. Easy to follow on this deer trail. They're headin' east o're the Sierras making an escape to their camp just under the peak. Likely they're camped over by that mountain lake, called Tahoe. Rough country, likely two-three days ride. We'll catch'm at their campsite."

Mike led the pair through the thick timber up into the mountains. The two horses never deviated from the deer trail. About mid-afternoon, Mike jumped from his horse and pulled a piece of white fabric stuck to the side of a deadfall branch that lay halfway into the path.

"What's that?" asked James. "How'd you even see that?"

"Looks to be a piece of Miss Trainer's petticoat, likely snagged as her horse passed by, observed Mike, as his eyes surveyed the surrounding area and the trail ahead.

"Then she's all right! Oh, I'm so thankful," James gushed.

"I'm afraid that conclusion is, …uh, premature," cautioned Mike, as he glanced their back trail. Mike swung his leg over the saddle and kicked his horse onward up the trail. "But it does suggest that we're on the right trail and that Jackson feller brought Miss Trainer along this same path. We're on the right track, my friend."

"I,…I just want to put my fist into their teeth," exclaimed James, as his right arm swung towards a low hanging branch.

Mike just shook his head, in disbelief. "Quiet, now, …never know when we might come upon their camp."

That night, Mike awoke when he heard one of the horses stamp and nicker. Mike grabbed his five-shot Colt Walker revolver, which he had picked up in a trade from a former Texas Ranger, and moved stealthily down the trail. He continued cautiously, listening, progressing slowly, a hundred yards, two hundred yards, slowly following the sound of the walking horse up ahead in the darkness. After nearly a quarter-mile up the steepening slope, he heard a rustling, a horse whinny and stumbling sound of hooves, then a thump and a groan, a hoarse whisper, and finally silence. Mike listened quietly, trying to distinguish the night time sounds of the forest, from the likely movement of the villains up ahead. Instincts suggested that James had foolishly ventured forth, on his own and was captured.

Soon, he came upon evidence that James, indeed, had been captured. In the partial moonlight, Mike could see bent and broken underbrush, and he felt the mix of horseshoe prints in the still damp soil. Then, there was a shiny reflection from the ground; James had dropped a pocket pistol in the tussle, that reflected in the dim moonlight. Mike picked up the weapon, and checked

It Takes a Woman

it for load and priming, and then slipped it into a small pocket on the upward inner side of his moccasin. Mike advanced cautiously, step by step, as the overhead sky lightened to a gray in the east just over the Sierra peaks.

"Hold it right there, stranger!" It was Ebenezer behind a tree, holding a flintlock rifle just three feet from Mike's head. Mike cursed to himself, angry that he had been so careless to be caught by a sentry.

"I'll take that mighty fine-looking pistol off your hands, mister. Handle first, very slowly."

In the background, Mike could now see James tied to a tree, with a gag in his mouth, shaking his head excitedly. Mike spun the Colt over and extended the handle towards the old coot, his finger still in the trigger guard. Ebenezer reached out for the pistol, and Mike was just then ready to flip his wrist to right the Colt when he was smacked from the rear behind his left knee, causing him to fall instantly and the pistol to fall to the ground.

He heard footsteps in the brush on the forest floor and looked up to see a small pocket pistol in his face and behind that a white sleeve and rotund figure of the gambler Leverette Laramore the Third.

"I only bet on sure things, mister trapper man, and when we caught that fool over there, I knew you'd be along shortly," Leverett gloated with his thumb in his red vest, looking down his nose at Mike laying at his feet. "I do believe, gentlemen, that we've just about got this project wrapped up."

"Boss!...Boss!" A third man appeared, running excitedly towards Leverett.

"Jackson! What the hell do you want?" barked Leverett as he turned towards the approaching man. "You're supposed to be watching the woman. Whaddya want?"

Jackson stopped suddenly, his mouth agape.

"Freeze all of you. Don't move fatso, or you're a dead man," barked a stern sounding female voice. Leverett jerked his plump torso as a rifle barrel was jammed into his back. "I'll take that Colt. Now anybody moves and he's a dead man. Think a lady can't shoot? Just try me!" It was Anne Trainer. Somehow in the ruckus of the men coming into the camp, she had escaped, and found a rifle and made it down the hill before Jackson realized she was gone.

Soon, Mike that the three villains tied, and ready to travel.

"Glad to see that you're all right Miss Trainer." Said Mike. "By the way, my name's Mountain Mike. Your family hired me to bring you back. I'm sure they'll be glad to see you."

Anne replied, "James, big brother, you're a bumbling fool once again. And you, Mr. Mountain Mike, while I appreciate your efforts, I'll have you know that I had things fully under control. Your little stumble as you entered camp did create a nice diversion; but I'll have you know that I was already free of my binds and ready to make my escape."

Then she smiled with a glint in her eye, "You men are all alike, thinking we women are so helpless. It seems to me, often as not, it takes a woman to do the job!"

##

Death Sentence

How will a gunslinger meet justice for his actions?

"Gentlemen of the jury, what is your verdict?"

The room became silent. Hesitantly, Joshua, a middle-aged farmer rose from the corner of the room, nervously holding a small slip of paper. He looked down, unfolded the paper, and then his eyes rose and scanned across the room and locked onto Johnny Floyd. Someone coughed over by the bar, and a glass clinked a little too hard onto a table in the back of the room.

In 1873, more often than not, justice in Kansas was meted out on the street. This time, because street justice had been perverted, justice was administered by a traveling circuit judge in the local saloon, the only room large enough to accommodate an angry citizenry. While the serving of whiskey was suspended during the trial, observers were permitted to consume drinks ordered before the trial began. On the western plains in July, a man needed liquid refreshment to make it through the day.

Joshua's jaw set, and a sneer formed on his lips. A chair shuffled in the crowded and stifling room. Outside, a horse whinnied and stamped its foot.

"The jury finds Johnny Floyd guilty," read juror Joshua, "guilty in the murder of Sarah Gorman… Death by hanging!" The roomful of angry citizens erupted, "Yeh! Yeh!" Above the din, one man yelled out, "Hang 'm from the ole oak tree!"

"I didn' do it! I didn' do it," an excited and fearful Johnny Floyd shouted, jumping to his feet, beads of nervous sweat forming on his forehead. Sheriff

Chase Chalmers pulled Floyd back to his seat and stepped between Floyd and the angry crowd.

BAM...BAM, the judge's gavel slammed onto the table, his authoritative voice booming, "Order! Silence or I'll clear this room!" The double click of a cocking shotgun carried over the din and quickly the crowd silenced.

"The community of Cimarron, in the State of Kansas, hereby declares that Johnny Floyd shall be put to death by hangin', a proper hangin'...to be carried out in five days," the judge's voice boomed out with authority. "But not on no damn oak tree. A proper hangin'. Sheriff Chalmers, you have 5 days in which to build a proper gallows, next to the jailhouse. This murderer, properly convicted, shall remain in your custody, and in 5 days at Noon, this order shall be carried out. This court is adjourned." BAM sounded the gavel.

Day One

After a sleepless night in his jail cell, a cell to which he was no stranger, Johnny lay on the hard cold bed, looking out at the gray dawn visible from the barred window across the one-room sheriff's office and jail. Sheriff Chalmers walked in carrying a cup of coffee, a delicious aroma filled the small room. The sparsely furnished room had a table in the center littered with some papers, coffee stains, and gun cleaning supplies. Two wooden chairs surrounded the table; a rifle rack was attached to one wall, and on the other wall was a faded map of the Kansas territory of the 1850s.

Situated on the remnants of the Santa Fe Trail, a major east-west pathway between central Missouri and the western town of Santa Fe, the community of Cimarron had grown as a stopping off point for western bound settlers. A roadhouse saloon was the first structure in the area, followed by several houses and farmsteads, and then a general store trading post. The community seemed to be an overflow outpost from nearby Dodge City, a town with a reputation for gunslingers and then gun slinging lawmen. Johnny Floyd had drifted into Cimarron after earning a reputation as a troublemaker with a quick-draw in Dodge; two deaths were attributed to Johnny's fast hand with a gun.

In his brief 23 years, Johnny was known for his drinking, gambling, fighting, and whoring. Sheriff Chalmers suspected Johnny was part of some cattle rustling and horse thieving, but that hadn't been proved. He never seemed to work, but he always seemed to have spending money, enough to come up with one of the new single action army Colts, the new six-gun with metal cartridges that was more reliable than the percussion revolvers in common use in the territory.

"Git up, Johnny," yelled Chase, "I'll not have you lying around all day." Johnny pushed his aching body upward, got his feet to the floor, and sat for a moment, scratching his head.

"Gimme some coffee, Chase," pleaded Johnny. Chase ignored Johnny's plea; he was watching as a wagon load of lumber was being brought up by a teamster from Dodge City. This was the lumber to be used for the gallows ordered by the judge. Johnny's plea continued, "Chase, I told ya I didn' do it. I told 'em all I didn' do it. It was that thieving Bobby Thompson, he done it."

"I seen the plans, Johnny," said Chase, ignoring Johnny's pleas. "They're building a mighty fine gallows, gonna hang you proper, jes like the judge said."

Johnny continued his denial. "Bobby Thompson, he done it. I just went in for a drink. Bobby started it. He accused me of taking his old sorrel mare… said it in front of all the guys. He can't talk to me that way. I couldn't just walk away, you know that Chase. He called me out to the street. You know, if you don't stand up to a guy like that, he'll run you out of the territory." Johnny thought he had Chase's attention. Now he continued, "We're standing there, I'm faster 'n' him, I knows it an' he knows it. An' then he's scared, and then this dog runs across the street 'tween us,…it came from over by the girl and the lady."

Johnny chokes and sobs as he recalls that day. "I didn' see no girl. She was just there, and then Bobby draws, he done it…I just reacted. Bobby shot her; I swear." Between sobs again he gasps, "I swear, Bobby done it. He shot her, wasn't my bullet."

Day Two

Johnny stirs on the hard jail cell bed, his sleep disturbed by the banging and hammering of two carpenters working in the lot next to the Cimarron jail. The folks of Cimarron, angry over the death of young Sarah, had all volunteered to help build the gallows that would put a proper end to the killer of a sweet young girl. Two with exceptional carpentry skills were selected.

Chase comes in again carrying that fine smelling coffee. Johnny is angry that his sleep was disturbed by the noisy pounding outside, and now his temper smolders. Knowing that Chase isn't about to share that fine smelling coffee, Johnny stands up, pushes his forehead against the jail bars, and swears. "Damn you, Chase, damn this town, damn that little dog and damn that little girl. Why me? I didn' do this. I tell ya Bobby done it."

All the times before, while Johnny had numerous scrapes with the law, he had avoided any real accountability. The several shootings, over Dodge City way, were questionable, but guns were drawn and Johnny remained standing while the other lay dead or dying. Johnny's pastimes were drinking and whoring, and gambling. After a few drinks, tempers seemed to flare, and fists would fly. But Johnny and his boys managed to escape with nothing more than a few bruises. No stranger to a jail cell, Johnny could either charm his way out or, a couple of times, his buddies might roust or threaten a witness who then seemed to not pursue the matter. But this time, someone innocent had died, a little girl and Johnny wasn't able to charm his way out. When the charm failed, his angry bully side emerged.

Johnny was on a roll, his face turning red as his anger grew. "My boys are comin' to get me…they'll break me outta here, you can't stop 'em, this place with its chintzy walls can't stop 'em. We busted my baby brother Frankie outta the Wichita jail last year.

Chase glanced at Johnny, then casually spat a wad of tobacco juice into the corner spittoon and said, "Shut up, Johnny, you're gonna get yours. A proper hangin, four more days!"

Day Three

A thunderstorm rolled through during the night. Flashes of lightning, followed by sharp booms of thunder kept Johnny awake half the night. By daylight, the storm's noise had eased, but steady rain continued throughout the day. No progress was made on the construction of the gallows. Waiting to die was taking its toll on Johnny. Nothing tasted good, what little he had eaten didn't sit well on his stomach. Three days of stubble around his chin was itchy, and Chase still did not share any of that fine smelling coffee.

The anger and threats from the preceding day had no effect on this sheriff. Johnny's mind raced faster and faster, trying to find a way out. Johnny pleaded his case again, this time from another angle, a bargain if he promised to be good. "Come on Chase, I tell ya Bobby done it. Jus' gimme one more chance. Tell that family I'm real sorry, I mean, I didn' do it, Bobby done it, I didn' mean it to happen that way. I'll do what I can to help that family. I been a good ranch hand and done farming too. I'd even take up religion, pray'n, and all that."

"You had a fair trial, Johnny," Chase replied. "All the facts came out, there was witnesses. Poor Sarah's mother was with her right there on the street. You coulda walked away. But you didn't. Witnesses seen it. You're gonna get yours this time, Johnny, fair and square." The day was quiet, folks pretty much stayed indoors, and the rain continued into the night.

Day Four

Somehow, Johnny had slept, and now a new day dawned. Nearby, a meadowlark warbled its flute-like song, and in the distance, a second bird answered. Not quite awake yet, and dreaming that he was sleeping on the hard prairie, Johnny felt free again, ready to ride into a new day. A door slammed and jolted Johnny awake.

Sitting up, he realized that he was still in the Cimarron jail on the hard bed. Suddenly, he felt very down, helpless, and depressed. There seemed to be no way out of this situation. The boys hadn't come, he was sure that little Frankie and his buddies would be coming around to spring him out of this little jail. But no one came, there was no word. Where were they? Didn't they care? Didn't anybody care?

Johnny felt weaker, sicker, and his back was still sore from the hard jail bed. He used to be a big eater, but the food didn't taste good and he wasn't hungry. The same four walls, and now today, that noisy banging and hammering were going on again outside. His thoughts seemed to materialize into words "That damn sheriff and that damn coffee, just to torture me, he brings it in every morning, smelling up the place but he won't let me have any. No one believes me...no one believes me."

Day Five

After a night of fitful sleep, Johnny lay facing the small window with the bars. A morning sunbeam slanted through the room visible because of the tiny golden dust particles that floated through the jailhouse. Somewhere in the distance, he heard that meadowlark warble once again. Today, that sound was calming, the meadowlarks were everywhere across the prairies of Kansas, but he hadn't noticed before. Today, though, the meadowlark's trill seemed to soothe his nerves. Outside, a horse whinnied, and its tail swished at a fly.

It was quiet outside. There was no more hammering. Johnny could hear a horse ride by, no it was two horses, and the riders were talking. For some reason, today, he felt calmer, more awake, more alert, more alive. Lying there, looking at the ceiling, he noticed a spider dangling on its web, a web that formed an angle from the ceiling to the wall, covering the corner. It occurred to Johnny, that spider must have been there all this time and he had not noticed it.

Now an aroma of coffee wafted in from the window, then he heard familiar sounding footsteps, footsteps of sheriff Chase. The door opened and Chase walked in, again carrying a cup of coffee. It smelled so good. The smell of coffee in the morning air seems to carry farther than at any other time of day. But wait, this time there were two cups and Chase reached through the bars and offered coffee to Johnny. Johnny accepted the coffee, and savored the aroma for more than a minute, before taking a sip.

Now it was time. Johnny stood quietly as Chase tied his hands behind his body, and led him from the jailhouse out towards the gallows in the lot next door. A crowd milled about, mostly men, but on the fringes, there were some women. Several children peaked from the corner of a nearby building or around a parked wagon. The women tried to shag the children away. As he was led to the stairs of the gallows, the crowd became quiet. It looked like most of the town showed up. Climbing the stairs, he noticed the fine carpentry work. The carpenters had done well.

Death Sentence

There was an "X" on the floor, and Chase led Johnny to stand on the "X." There was a trap-door cut-out surrounding the "X" and below he could see the sandy tan-colored soil of the Kansas plains. A hundred eyes looked up at him. Johnny marveled that his breathing was calm and even. A noose was placed around his neck and slid firm, but not tight.

Johnny closed his eyes, and in his mind, he saw that day, that day in front of the saloon, where he and Bobby had words. Both had drinks and were quick to anger. Then they were standing in the street, face to face, about 60 feet between them. Johnny had shot others like this before, he knew he was fast, he knew he could beat Bobby.

But then this dog ran between them. It all came back to Johnny's mind in a flash. Bobby's eyes followed the dog, Johnny knew he could beat Bobby and he drew and fired. But suddenly as he fired, he saw this little girl. In a split second, she spun and fell, and then lay there. Then a puddle of blood seemed to ooze from the ground under her. To his left, a woman was screaming.

Johnny opened his eyes, and at the back of the crowd, he saw Sarah's mother and father. His eyes closed again, as he thought, "I done it. I done wrong." Then he heard an Ax chop into a rope and the floor opened up.

# #

Donovan's Dream

Will a California man succeed in finding the killer of his wife?

Donald Donovan woke with a start, with a vivid memory of the painful screams of his wife, Kathleen. He looked around, in a grey fog, again hearing high pitched screech. Up the hill he saw a ringtail, half out of its hole, squealing noisily. To his left, down the hill, he heard a rustling sound, a momentary flash of movement, showing reddish-brown fur, which he recognized as a fox chasing another ringtail into the safety of its hole in the ground. That one got away, but the fox would find another.

The pounding pain in his head and the ache in his back from sleeping on the hard ground caused his thinking to be as thick and foggy as the morning sky above. He shivered momentarily, feeling the dampness of his clothes and the cool air overhead. An awareness crept into his mind, assembling some of the events of the previous night. The rig was parked and the horses stabled. Then, he had ridden the dun bareback to the saloon in Marysville. Whiskey, it seemed, was the only thing that pushed Kathleen's painful cries from his memory.

Bartender Kevin, who hailed from the Kilkenny area of Ireland where the Donovan family shared roots, would tolerate Donovan's self-loathing anger brought on by the third or fourth whiskey. Other patrons of the saloon, however, were tired after their day's labor and had little tolerance for the rants of a drunken Irishman mourning his lot in life.

Donovan's Dream

"Time to head for home, Donovan, you've had your limit," suggests Kevin, as he places the whiskey bottle on the shelf back behind the bar.

"…need another," mumbles Donovan, his tongue now thick from a fourth glass of whiskey," in memory of me lovely wife,… bonnie Kathleen." As he held out his glass for another pour, his balance slipped and he bumped into the man standing next to him at the bar.

The bump spilled the whiskey in the hand of the next drinker, an action which was instinctively met by a swinging fist, landing squarely on Donovan's jaw. Jarred backward, Donovan stumbled falling onto a table scattering cards, money, gold nuggets and more spilled whiskey as the table collapsed from his 180 pounds of solid teamster muscles. Now, four more angry drunks joined the melee and piled into Donovan, each getting in a punch or kick before Kevin came around the bar with a two-foot oak club.

Now here he was, on a foggy hillside, under an oak tree next to a rocky creek bed with a throbbing head and sore back. He stood slowly, and his eyes surveyed the terrain. More memory returned, as he realized, he was near the base of North Butte. When the whiskey wasn't working, a lonely walk through the Buttes seemed to be his only sanctuary to try to bury the painful memories of loss and hopes for what might have been.

The Buttes were a collection of small mountains rising from the central California plains, about 5 miles west of Marysville. The Maidu Indians, original residents of this area, had regarded the area as a spiritual place. Though the Maidu had been driven from the area by the white settlers during the gold rush in the 1850s, Donovan felt the spirits and serenity of the area when he walked into the region and climbed the hills. Huge boulders were scattered about, boulders as large as a wagon, or even a small cabin. Old-timers said that the area had been formed by a volcano of exploding rock and soil. Donovan couldn't imagine such an explosion.

Donovan shivered again in the damp fog, then shook it off, and began his climb. Following alongside the creek bed, ascending the hill, Donovan found a wildlife trail, barely visible, marked only by hoof print ridges in the soil when larger animals like deer or an occasional strayed cow walked in the area in search of grasses to eat. The ascending hill became steeper, and the presence of the live oak and blue oak trees became thinner and more scattered, giving way to mesquite brush and juniper clinging to the rock. More of the base rock and boulders were present, causing Donovan to use hands and feet to find footholds and to climb up and around the boulders.

Breathing heavily, with his heart pounding from the exertion of a near-vertical climb, Donovan now saw the fog begin to break as sunbeams sloped through from the eastern sky. With the fog now clearing, a Turkey vulture soared in circles off to his left, some 1500 feet over the valley below where he lay moments ago, the huge bird likely monitoring the activities of the fox and hoping for some leftovers after the hard work was done.

The final 100 feet near the peak was a vertical stone escarpment, with crevices, causing Donovan to sweat as he inched upward finding cracks for hand and toe holds. Reaching a level spot near the top, he sat and surveyed the surrounding vista. A river meandered to the west, lined by trees and filled with flocks of ducks, and to the east, the dark gray Sierra Nevada mountain range loomed.

Again, thoughts of his lovely wife Kathleen again consume Donovan's mind. Just 18 when she died, she had been shot and mortally wounded by a band of outlaws coming down from the gold claims in the mountains. Kathleen and her sister Coleen had set up a tent along the roadway north of Marysville, to prepare home-cooked meals for travelers heading to mining sites in the mountains to the north and east.

Donovan recalled that morning a year ago, on the last day he had seen Kathleen healthy and alive. It was a sunny day, with warm breezes of the early California spring spreading the fragrant aromas of the spring blossoms along the roadway. Donovan had kissed Kathleen good -by as she worked at the food preparation table at the back of the tent, her hands dusty with flour after mixing dough for the biscuits, saying, "just one trip to Sacramento, then over to Hangtown, and I should be back in three days." She had given him a kiss, a smile, and a wink, saying, "stay safe," and then pushed him out of the way, leaving white handprints on his shirt.

Donovan's Dream

Donovan had returned to the tent after completing the three-day delivery loop. As he approached the tent, he heard a gunshot and then a scream…a scream that sounded like Kathleen. There was a commotion, and then two men raced by pushing their horses hard towards the south. He caught a glance of them, dirty looking saddle tramps, un-shaven and grimy from living in the hills. One seemed young and skinny, while the other had a bull neck with shoulders and arms built from stevedore work handling heavy merchandise much like Donovan's own work as a teamster. Donovan walked around the corner and then found Kathleen on the ground, head in the lap of sister Coleen, bleeding from a gaping wound in her stomach. Donovan had held her for a few moments before her breathing stopped and her eyes stared lifelessly at the sky above. All he heard then were the wails of their two-year-old daughter, Mary Katherine.

In the days that followed, Donovan had been in a daze, numb from the unexpected loss of Kathleen. With Kathleen's death, so too had died Donovan's dream. He and Kathleen had planned to work hard, her at the food tent and he with the deliveries, in order to build their lives in this new land, maybe even buy a ranch. Now that was all gone. Kathleen's little sister, 16-year-old Coleen, had valiantly stepped in to care for little Mary Katherine all the while continuing to run the food tent. After Kathleen's burial, Donovan had pushed himself to return to his teamster work making deliveries of merchandise and supplies from the Sacramento docks to the mining areas and in the nearby communities of Marysville, Auburn, Hangtown, and up to Oroville.

Since that moment, a year ago, Donovan existed, but his life had stopped; without his life partner and their dream, his life was meaningless. Donovan just went through the motions, doing his job as a teamster, delivering wagon loads and then stopping off at the Marysville tavern to wash away the painful memories that continued to haunt him, the memory of Kathleen dying in his arms.

One day, while picking up a load from the docks in Sacramento, the movements of a stevedore caught his eye. It was a bull of a man, unloading barrels from a steamboat, possessing the strength to pick up a 200-pound barrel, hoist it to his shoulder, and carry it to another teamster wagon. Donovan observed the man's profile, his bull-like neck, strong shoulders, and tree trunk arms, hoisting boxes and barrels like they were empty, loading another wagon about 20 yards away. Twice, Donovan lost track of the merchandise being placed into his own wagon, and he had to re-count items against the bill of lading.

Then another man, a skinny one, rode up and tied his horse to a nearby hitching rail. The skinny man walked over and began talking to the stevedore as he finished loading the other wagon and pointing over to the horse. Now, the hair stood up on the back of Donovan's neck, and his memory flashed back to that awful day a year ago. He recalled the commotion, two riders, one skinny with toothpick arms and another bull –neck, both racing away, and then coming upon his lovely Kathleen, her life-blood flowing from her midsection, pale with her lips quivering as she whispered a final 'I love you.' Donovan's muscles tensed, fists forming in each hand, his jaw set and nostrils flaring as his breathing intensified.

"Donovan…You're loaded. This load goes to Auburn. Now git your wagon off my dock!" yelled the yardmaster. Donovan spun around, his right fist drawing back, ready to spring a knock-out punch when he saw 20 yards behind the yardmaster the skinny man shaking the reins of his wagon to spur his team out of the yard. Donovan's eyes circled the dock and he saw the bull neck man mounting the horse left by the skinny one, and riding off towards the center of Sacramento. "Move it," repeated the Yardmaster, "I've got wagons waiting."

Donovan jumped up to the hard wooden seat of his wagon, pulled the lever to release the brake, and yelled "Hee-yaa…hee-yaa," as he shook the reins over the backs of his team. The wagon lurched forward and Donovan steered the team in the same direction as the skinny driver, now about a block ahead, going east out towards Hangtown. Donovan knew he'd never catch the single rider, but he could easily catch the skinny driver and his wagon. About a mile out of Sacramento, Donovan pulled up within 100 yards behind the skinny driver.

The roadway was lightly traveled. Since leaving Sacramento, only one rider had passed by heading into town. *I could take this guy out right here, right now,* thought Donovan, struggling to rein in his Irish temper and his urge to take an eye for an eye. In the 1850s in the central California gold rush era, there was no sheriff or lawman like they had back east. Here, you wore the law strapped to your belt, whether it be a pistol or knife, or carried a flintlock rifle.

Thinking and planning, Donovan considered: *I've got to be smart about this, I didn't see who killed Kathleen, I only saw two men riding away. This skinny man and his bull-neck friend certainly look like the ones I saw riding away that day, but it was only for a second or two.* Then, Donovan remembered, *Coleen was there that day and she must have seen them. I've got to describe them to Coleen to see if they're the ones, maybe even find a way to let Coleen have a look at them. Then I'll deal with 'em,... make 'em pay.*

Donovan reached down to the small box under his wagon seat and pulled up a pistol which he slipped under his belt, on his left side. Then he slapped the reins to spur his team to catch the skinny driver. "Yo teamster,...hellooo," called Donovan. Catching the other wagon, he pulled onto the left side of the pathway so that the other driver couldn't see the pistol in his belt. The other driver finally heard Donovan's team approach and turned looking surprised, his mouth dropping open.

" Hey man…Ye headin' up to Jamison's trading post in Hangtown?" Donovan queried.

" Huh? Oh, … yeh," the skinny one replied hesitantly in a high pitched nasally voice.

The good Lord didn't bless this one with body, mind, or voice, thought Donovan, *definitely a follower, not a leader.* "You work for Smythe? I know Smythe runs a lot of wagons out of Sacramento up into the hills."

"Uh…. Yeh, … Smythe, Yeh."

" I thought I recognized the brand on your team. Saw you get loaded down by the docks, … with a big fella hoofin' the load, he a Smythe man too?" queried Donovan.

"Huh? …uh,… no, …Seamus…he's my cuzzin. Found me this job, We was working in the hills, but had to move on."

Seamus, thought Donovan, *damned if he's not another Irishman,… but I'll have at 'im if he's the one.* "I haul for Kaufman, out of Marysville. Kaufman says he's lookin' for a stevedore. Where does this Seamus hang his hat?"

"Huh?… Oh, Seamus an' me got a little place west of the river, 'bout a,…'bout a mile from Sacramento," intoned the nasally reply.

With that, Donovan pulled left on the reins to steer his team in a northerly direction on the cut-off towards Auburn, another of the new gold rush mining towns popping up in the Sierra Nevada foothills. Donovan finished his load and then headed back towards the stable in Marysville. No stopping at the bar this night; for the first time in a long time, Donovan felt like he had a purpose. He had a lead on Kathleen's killer and he wanted to have Coleen have a look to see if she recognized the men who attacked Kathleen.

The next Sunday morning, after an early breakfast at sunrise, Donovan and Coleen were in the wagon and on the road south to Sacramento. It was a two-day trip, stopping first at a boarding house near the Nicolaus Landing ferry which crossed the Feather River. By mid-afternoon the next day, they had reached Sacramento and were crossing the river on the ferry to look for Seamus' place. The ferry-man, prompted by the gift of a small bottle of whiskey from Donovan, freely recalled knowing Seamus, "… and his skinny cousin Colin. I hate the sound of his squeaky voice. They're trouble-makers, twice they've stiffed me on the ferry fee,… get on the ferry drunk of a Saturday night making trouble with me other customers, and the big one Seamus is a real bully, ain't no stoppin' him after a nite of drinkin'. Got themselves a log and mud-brick shack 'bout a mile down the road towards 'Frisco. I'd be careful about messin' with the big one."

After a short ride down the road, Donovan saw the log and mud shack ahead, and he steered the team into a small clearing behind a stand of trees near a creek. From there, he could watch the shack without being seen by its occupants or by travelers coming down the road. Donovan cut a small branch from a tree and swished away the hoof and wheel marks where they had turned off the road. He tied the horses where they could munch on some grass, and brought out a packed lunch for Coleen and himself. They found a spot on a log where they had a view of the approaching roadway and the shack.

Donovan's Dream

After an hour or so, Donovan heard a ruckus from the roadway, two riders, cursing, yelling, with a horse snorting and whinnying in reaction to mean treatment, probably by the rider. Donovan alerted Coleen, and they watched as the riders approached. The big one, Seamus, clearly drunk, rode by jerking the reins of his horse, kicking its ribs and slapping its side with a leather riata, cursing at the animal and cursing at his companion, cousin Colin.

Donovan felt his muscles tense with anger watching Seamus mistreat the animal, but he held back, remembering that his purpose today was to see if Coleen recognized either man as the ones who had killed Kathleen that fateful day.

"That's him! There's the other one. That's them…they're the ones what killed Kathleen," whispered Coleen excitedly, looking quickly to Donovan and back towards the riders. "They were drunk, just like this, and that big one comes in the tent where we're preparing dinner, and…and…he's cursing like this and he's bothering a couple of early customers."

Tears begin to flow down Coleen's cheeks as she recalls that day, her voice getting higher pitched becoming broken by sobs, "…and,…and Kathleen says just sit and we'll serve you. She,…she was always calm and good with the customers, and that big one bumps a table and spills this man's dinner, and he gets up angry, and Kathleen steps between them to stop a fight and…and then there's a shot. And they run out and I hear horses. Then you came in…Oh Donovan, it was just awful." Donovan quickly pulls Coleen to him and buries her sobs into his chest and arms.

It was a long silent ride back to their place in Marysville, the silence broken only by Coleen's quiet sobs and sniffles as she struggled with the awful memories of that day a year ago. Donovan's mind, likewise, was a jumbled mess of anger and spite, as he considered various scenarios in which he would right this wrong. The man's barrel chest and tree-trunk arms and neck probably gave him a 50-pound edge on Donovan's 180-pound lean teamster frame. But it made no difference, this man,…these men,… had destroyed Donovan's dream, his dream of a happy life with the lovely Kathleen.

Donovan had always prepared for danger when he traveled. The trip across the great plains several years before, threatened by bands of marauding

Indians, had taught him to always travel with two more weapons, like a gun and a knife. When he began working as a teamster, he routinely carried a knife on his belt, a second knife in his right boot, and a pistol, either on his belt or in the storage box under his wagon seat. But now, he came across one of the new Colt dragoon five-shot revolvers, similar to the ones used by the famed Texas Rangers. It cost him a week's pay, but he would be ready.

Several weeks later, on a Friday evening, after a day of deliveries between the Sacramento docks and the trading posts in the hill country, Donovan found himself pulling his wagon to a stop at a road-house tavern between Auburn and Sacramento. A couple of other teamster rigs were tied outside, along with several horses. From the sound of the voices, boisterous talk, and loud laughter, the travelers inside had a head start on dulling the pain of the workweek. As he secured his team at a nearby hitching post, the sounds inside grew in intensity and changed from laughter to argument.

Such talk was common when men gathered and drank whiskey. Donovan knew full well, having had a few tussles and a punch or two in reply to a whiskey induced insult. As he stepped toward the door, furniture crashed inside and a man with a white apron around his waist came flying awkwardly headfirst out the door landing against Donovan and knocking both to the ground. Donovan rolled away and Jumped up expecting a punch from the man with the apron, but then he sensed movement from his right, as another figure quickly emerged from the roadhouse door and jumped onto the first man, pummeling him with his massive fists. Donovan quickly assessed the situation, recognizing the attacker as the bull neck Seamus, beating up on the roadhouse bartender, a man half his size.

Donovan reached in with his left, grabbed Seamus' shoulder pulling him off of the bartender, and followed quickly with a solid right hook to the charging man's jaw. Donovan could feel a tooth give and saw a bit of blood at the hunk's lips. Seamus reacted with a grunt but quickly recovered with a roundhouse that sent Donovan spinning. Donovan was quickly set upon by Seamus, and the two exchanged a series of close body jabs to the chest and chin. Donovan became aware of others behind him, the roadhouse drinkers now cheering the fight.

Donovan's Dream

Now with an audience, Seamus seemed to show off and wound up for a right hook. In that half a second wind-up, Donovan stepped in with a left to the hunk's stomach, knocking out the bigger man's wind and stumbling him backward. As Donovan stepped in for a follow-up punch, he heard a shot from behind that hit his left arm, spinning him to the ground. Following his spinning movement on the ground, Donovan instinctively reached for his Colt, drew, and fired at a skinny man holding the smoking gun pointed in his direction.

Still crouched, Donovan saw a metal glint from his left where he had seen Seamus gasping for a breath. Now, two guns spit fire simultaneously, and Donovan felt the heat of a bullet pass his ear, but saw Seamus recoil backward, with a red blotch growing on his chest. Seamus attempted to pull his pistol up for a second shot, then his mouth dropped open, as his face paled to a dull gray color and his eyes looked down at the gun in his hand. The gun discharged into the ground and Seamus fell forward, headfirst into the dust.

The circle of men stood silently, looking at Donovan, and back to the two men who had first beat up the bartender and then tried to kill a good Samaritan who had interceded in an unfair fight.

"Thank you for helping me," said the bartender, his nose bloodied. "Let me offer you a drink on the house."

"Huh? No, I gotta go."

Only then, did Donovan fully recognize that he had stopped Seamus and Colin, the killers of the lovely Kathleen. Donovan now thought of baby Mary Katherine, and how he would focus on raising her right to fulfill the dream he had shared with Kathleen.

##

Selling Out

Is there honor among thieves?

"This is a hold-up! Everybody against the wall…over there…Now!" yelled Tawny.

Three customers at the teller windows turned quickly, backing away from the gruff-looking dusty brute waving a Colt. Gasps were heard, and one woman holding a parasol that matched her floor-length royal blue taffeta dress let out a fearful shriek.

Trail dirty, big-boned with solid muscles, and a pocked complexion, Tawny looked threatening with or without a brandished Colt. The tellers, two middle-aged men in white shirts with high collars and sleeve guards, instinctively raised their hands.

One customer, a trail worn cattleman, turned slowly, his right hand dropping to his holstered pistol. BAM. Tawny's Colt spit fire, the cattleman lurched back half a step, his left hand leaning on the teller window ledge, and the right hand in mid-draw, dropped the pistol to the floor. The cattleman slumped forward and fell face-first to the floor of the Emporia Bank. Another shriek arose from the parasol lady, who fainted dead away.

There was a moment of dead silence as all eyes fixed on the body, slumped on the bank floor, with blood pooling around the man's chest.

"Now you went an' done it…jeez, … Tawny. Ya said there'd be no killin'.", pleaded a winey voice from just inside the door. He too held a Colt, but the pistol shook in his nervous hand. He was barely old enough to show

Selling Out

whiskers, a bit pudgy, with unruly blond hair that hung into his face and over his shirt collar. "Ya said we'd get the money quick like an' get out."

"Shut up Curly," yelled Tawny. He waved his gun, threatening the tellers, then tossing a canvas bag behind the bars at the teller window. "Money in this bag,...fill it now!" He turned to Curly and barked, "Those customers...get their money, jewelry, guns. Put it in that bag he's got. Now! Or you'll end up like that one on the floor."

Their bags filled, the robbers backed to the doorway, waving their Colts, and quickly stepped into the street and mounting their horses, which were being held by a third member guarding outside. They spurred their horses west, out of Emporia, one of the towns formed in the settling of the new state of Kansas.

The robbers rode hard for the first five miles, with no words spoken, putting miles between them and Emporia. Tawny saw a creek bed ahead on the right and directed the riders into the wooded area and along the creek. They walked their horses in the rocky creek bed for maybe half a mile and then crossed over into grassy plains of eastern Kansas. They rode down into a draw and continued in a northwesterly direction.

The third rider held back at the creek momentarily to water his horse and take a drink. After a few moments, he caught up with Tawny and Curly.

"When we gonna stop?" wined Curly. "My horse is beat. I'm plum wore out, an' need a drink. Why didn't we stop for a drink in that creek?"

Tawny shared an aggravated glance with Johnny Webb, the third member of the group. "Shut up Curly," barked Tawny. "They'll be coming after us. This is no time to stop. We'll stop after dark." He spurred the horse back up to a canter, after a brief rest from walking along the creek bed. When the golden prairie dusk faded to near darkness, Tawny reigned up near a stand of willows along another creek bed.

"No fires. Water the horses an' rub them down," ordered Tawny. His very demeanor was threatening, demanding action of others. Curly, youngest of the three, instantly obeyed. Johnny Webb, arms on his hips, close to the low slung tied down Colts at each side stood his ground facing Tawny head-on and didn't move.

"Time for the split," says Johnny. "I done my part. Clean get-away. Nothin' sloppy like what happened inside." At 26, Johnny was a seasoned outlaw. Johnny's reputation included horse and cattle rustling, hitting a stagecoach, and he was credited with a trail of bodies through Kansas and Missouri. Johnny had met Tawny when they did time in Leavenworth two years ago. Though of smaller stature, Johnny knew not to back down from Tawny's gruff bluster.

"All-right. All-right," says Tawny. "I'm counting it out now. It'll be a quarter for each of you." Curly appeared, eager for his share, saying nothing about the uneven split. Johnny glared at Tawny, his hand hovering near the Colt. Tawny replied with further bluster, "I ram-rod this outfit. My job, I call the shots. Take was four thousand. You each get a thousand," as he sorted and pushed the pile of cash towards Curly and Johnny. As Curly eagerly scooped up his loot and turned away, Tawny pushed an extra pile of bills towards Johnny, with a gesture to say keep this between us.

In the days that followed, the three traveled north and west through Kansas, stopping at each small town saloon along the way, for whiskey, cards, and any opportunity for easy pickings. If the card game didn't go their way, the winner usually ended up with a knock on the head and his pockets emptied as he headed home from a night of drinking. Other times, Johnny and Tawny would try a scam at cards, pretending to be strangers, but making subtle gestures to the other when they got a lead on a hand.

But at the end of the night, it always seemed to be the same issue, Tawny tried to hold out the lion's share and throw crumbs to Johnny and Curly. Being a bit slow, and a follower, Curly followed orders, took his cut, and seemed satisfied to be part of the gang, not realizing he was being cheated by his "friends."

Tawny and company made the rounds in eastern Kansas, up to Council Grove for a few days, then on the road again. But whenever it was time to make the split, Tawny always insisted on his half. Curly accepted his crumbs, but it ate at Johnny's craw, because, as often as not, he was the winner at cards,

Selling Out

or knocked heads in the ally-ways or behind the stables. One night, Johnny stood up to Tawny, and fists flared. Tawny's size and strength, overcame Johnny's speed and agility, resulting in a pummeling that was broken up by a tearful Curly, upset that his friends were fighting.

The next stop was Junction City. The young soldiers from nearby Fort Riley were easy marks, either in saloon card games or in the ally-ways after a night of drinking and gambling. Despite the ruckus at Council Grove, Tawny continued to claim his "share." Johnny was careful to confront Tawny only when his Colts were handy and Curly was occupied elsewhere. With the odds tipped in his favor, Johnny could get an extra split from Tawny.

One night, while drinking at a Junction City saloon, Johnny overheard a cattle broker talking of a cash shipment due in from Topeka to cover payouts and payroll for cattle drive due into Abilene in a few days. Maybe, Johnny thought, this'll be the big score. I can catch this and be done with these guys. The next day, Johnny hung out by the livery stable to listen to the palaver about the incoming stage. Then he rode out east of town to check the roadway to find a suitable spot for a hold-up.

He found a narrow pass on the roadway east towards Topeka, about 5 miles out of town. As he circled the area, he heard an Army supply wagon with riders approaching. He ducked into the brush and watched the wagon pass. Upon return to their hideout near town, Johnny decided that he need a hand in pulling off this job, so he'd tell Tawny and Curly. But this was his job and he'd call the split.

"Yeh, ...Ych, ... sure," said Tawny upon hearing about the job and the setup. "It'll be your show. Think you can handle it, kid?"

"I call the job ...an' I call the split," puffed Johnny, his fists tightening and his chin sticking out in determination.

The day came, and Johnny led the group out to the narrow draw, instructing each where to set up and wait. "On my signal," says Johnny, "should be along about 2:00. We got half an hour." But 2:00 dragged on to 2:30 and then to 3:00, with no stage. Across the way, Johnny could see Tawny's horse dancing nervously, and Tawny doing nothing to calm the animal. Johnny stepped from behind the tree stump and waved his hat in a downward motion to signal Tawny to calm the horse down.

"It's comin'…its comin'" an excited Curly yelled in a hoarse whisper that could be heard across the roadway. Johnny waved his hat to silence his partners. In a few moments, they heard the clop of the team and the creaks and jolts of the stage as it bounced along the packed dirt roadway. As the stage rounded the bend in the road, Johnny spurred his horse in front of the stage and fired a shot in the air.

"Hold it right there. You're covered. Don't try anything," yelled Johnny, waving both Colts in the air and then settling his aim on the guard. "Drop that shotgun. Both of you…guns on the ground." By that time, Tawny had approached from the other side, and Curly appeared at the rear, each with Colts drawn.

There was a movement from inside the coach. Tawny's Colt jerked and fired, causing a surprised curse from inside, and the stage lurched as its team reacted to the shot. "Throw your guns out, and come out with your hands up," yelled Tawny.

Two guns dropped to the ground, and then a woman, a boy climbed out quickly, and then slowly a man stumbled out holding a bleeding shoulder. All eyes were turned as the man fell to the ground next to the stage. From behind the stage, a winey voice said, "good shootin' Tawny."

Tawny had control now and he knew it. His take-charge instinct continued, as he pointed the Colt at the guard. "The payroll box,…now!…throw it down." The guard hesitated momentarily, and Tawny fired a shot just missing the guard but sending his hat flying in the breeze. This spurred action as the guard and driver reached under their seat and pulled up a heavy trunk and pushed it out onto the ground. The team lurched a step, startled by the falling trunk.

Tawny kept the momentum of the situation. "You people get back in that stage, get that stupid one in there, don't try anything stupid or you'll get a bullet too!" As the passengers scrambled back in, Tawny put a shot at the feet of the team yelling "Hee-yaa, hee-yaa. Get that wagon outta here." The stage

Selling Out

lurched forward, and Tawny put another shot over their heads for good measure.

By now Johnny had jumped off his horse and was struggling with the strong-box trunk. It was solid oak, with brass corners, about 2 feet on each side, and must have weighed close to 150 – 200 pounds secured by a big padlock. Even with metal handles on each side. Johnny could not get it up or secured on his horse.

Tawny again sized up the situation, barking an order, "Curly, bring your horse over here. Take this rope, Tie it through those handles. Now the two of you lift that thing by the ropes and tie them to the pommels. Come – on. Times a wasting. Let's go this way. We're cutting south. We can't take this into town, you idiots."

Following Tawny, they had to walk the horses side by side, while the trunk swung between them. At one point, Curly tried to ride, but the horses resisted the extra weight, so they ended up walking along with the horses, as Tawny rode and lead the way. Tawny led them into a creek and marched them along in the water for about a quarter mile before crossing to the other side.

By nightfall they had covered maybe 8 or 10 painful aching miles, as they circled to the west of Junction City. "No fires," announced Tawny, "They'll be out looking for us. Could be anywhere."

Johnny was fidgeting with the lock, and in frustration, he reached for his Colt. "And no guns either," growled Tawny as he grabbed Johnny's wrist. "They'll hear a shot just like they'll see a fire. Ya wanna send a beacon to tell them where we are?"

They continued for three more days until they were near the cow town of Abilene. There they camped in the woods along the Smokey Hill River. "All right, let's open it up," says Tawny, rubbing his hand together. He went to his saddle boot and brought back a 50 caliber Sharps rifle, a buffalo gun. "Back off you two, this might spit back at us," Tawny cautioned.

BOOM. The first shot spun the padlock doing more damage to their ears than the nick on the lock's plate. Again,…BOOM and the lock's arm shattered.

They all converged, hands reaching in to open the trunk. They pulled up the lid and revealed a trunk full of bills, federal notes, and coins in gold and silver.

"Wooo-hoo, Wooo-hoo," yelled Johnny and Curly. Their celebration was interrupted by the BAM of Tawny's Colt. Curly froze, his mouth agape, as he backed up. Johnny's hand moved towards his Colt, only to have it slapped away by the barrel of Tawny's Colt. Johnny, too backed away, seeing that Tawny had the drop on them. Johnny's temper sizzled, his jaw set, as he growled, "this was my job, my split. I told you."

Negotiating with others is easy when you hold the gun. Speaking calmly, while gesturing with his Colt, Tawny said, "and you blew it, you lost control, we nearly got shot, I stopped that stupid one in the stage. And then I had to save your ass because you couldn't even pick up the trunk. I saved this job. I call the splits. I got the gun and my gun has spoken."

At the end of the night, they had counted out eight thousand dollars, and again, Tawny called the split, "four for me, and two for each of you." Curly, as usual, was happy with his share, and again, Johnny was stewing, but he knew he couldn't get the drop on Tawny. With money in camp, Tawny slept like a lynx, ever alert with one eye open.

With this score, the group made it to Abilene, ready for partying, drinking, gambling and whoring. The next day, Johnny saw a wanted poster as he passed by the Sheriff's office. There it was, a sketch of Tawny, with the notice: *Wanted – Dead or Alive. Thomas "Tawny" Cragin wanted for murder and bank Robbery in Emporia Kansas. Known accomplice: "Curly" young man with blond hair. $1000 Reward.*

Johnny thought, *the law…they don't know about me.* Johnny had stopped next at the general store, picking up some coffee and ammunition. While there, he observed two women shopping and talking, one dressed in black, in mourning.

"You've been such a savior, dear sister, taking me in these days after those hooligans killed Carl," said the widow.

Selling Out

"It's so awful, sweet sister, of course, we're here for you. Stay as long as you like. I'm glad to see that the Emporia Bank put up a reward. I hope they catch those hooligans," replied the other.

Moments later, outside the store, Johnny tipped his hat, and said, "Mornin' ladies, pardon me for interrupting, and deepest sympathies. I hear tell that the men that done that awful deed, they're camped east of town out by the Smokey Hill River. Maybe the sheriff would like to know."

"Dear man," says the widow, "I'll tell the sheriff right away. When they catch those two hooligans, I'll see that you get that reward."

##

William S. Hubbartt

Publication credits

The short stories featured in Live or Die by the Gun first appeared in various western themed E-zines.

It Takes a Woman, Death Sentence, Donovan's Dream, and Selling Out first appeared at Rope and Wire.Com.

The Last Score, Fool's Gold, Caleb's Courage, Spirit of Sonora, Hell and High Water first appeared at Frontier Tales.com.

Soldier's Heart first appeared at thebigadios.com.

Portions of Live or Die by the Gun first appeared as E-books entitled Death on the Santa Fe Trail and The Last Score, first published by Outlaws Publishing LLC.

Author William S. Hubbartt holds all original copyrights for these works. All stories have been reprinted with permission.

About the Author

William S. Hubbartt is author of fiction and non-fiction works. Hubbartt is author of various fiction short story placements which have appeared in Zimbell House Ghost Stories Anthology, No Trace Anthology, Storyteller Anthology Magazine, Mondays are Murder, Heater E-fiction Magazine, Wilderness House Literary Review, www.FrontierTales.com, Ropeandwire.com and Thebigadios.com. Additional publication credits include 5 non-fiction books on business related topics, numerous articles in professional magazines and trade journals. Mr. Hubbartt's employment spans industry, government, human resources consulting and education. His current employment focuses on writing and human resources consulting.

William S. Hubbartt

List of Books by William S. Hubbartt

Western Fiction

Live and Die by the Gun 2021

Lawman's Justice 2020 *

Justice for Abraham 2020*

Six Bullet Justice 2020*

Blazing Guns on the Santa Fe Trail 2020

*First appeared as E-books under Outlaws Publishing LLC label

Crime & Mystery Fiction

Drawing a Line: A look inside the corporate response to sexual harassment 2020

Non-fiction

Achieving Performance Results: Boosting Performance in the Virtual workplace 2019

HIPPA Privacy Sourcebook 2004

The HIPPA Security Rule 2004

The Medical Privacy Rule 2002

The New Battle Over Workplace Privacy 1998

Personnel Policy Handbook: How do develop a manual that works 1993

Performance Appraisal Manual for Managers and Supervisors 1992

Printed in Great Britain
by Amazon